Chaos in the cantina . . .

A ...
ing ...
a ma...
Buff...

H...
the I...
eyes...
dit's...
stop ...

RIDERS

OF THE MONTE

L. J. Washburn

BERKLEY BOOKS, NEW YORK

RIDERS OF THE MONTE

A Berkley Book / published by arrangement with
the author

PRINTING HISTORY
M. Evans and Company, Inc., edition / February 1990
Berkley edition / June 1998

ISBN: 0-425-16374-1

BERKLEY®
Berkley Books are published by
The Berkley Publishing Group, a member of Penguin Putnam Inc.,
200 Madison Avenue, New York, New York 10016.
BERKLEY and the "B" design
are trademarks belonging to Berkley Publishing Corporation.

PRINTED IN THE UNITED STATES OF AMERICA

10 9 8 7 6 5 4 3 2 1

To Renea and those Texas summer days

RIDERS
OF THE MONTE

P R O L O G U E

ONE THING ABOUT BOUNDARY lines, Curtis Daniels thought as he twisted a little in his saddle in an attempt to ease his aching back, they didn't mean a whole hell of a lot when it came to the weather. It was just as hot and dry and dusty here in Mexico as it had ever been across the border in Texas.

Daniels lifted his pale blue eyes to the foothills at the edge of the Los Caballos plains. The hills faded back to the west, gradually rising and turning into the Sierra Madre. Tall, cool grayish-blue mountains were a pretty sight to a man plodding along through these flat, arid wastes. But it was mighty frustrating to see those mountains and know that you could ride for days and days and still not be anywhere near them.

Glancing around him, Daniels saw that he was the only one of the bandits who had his head up—except for Guerrero. Ignacio Guerrero was always alert, his dark eyes darting around for any sign of a potential threat. The *bandido* chieftain rode with his right hand resting on his thigh, only inches away from the butt of his Navy Colt. Guerrero could pull the gun in a hurry if he needed to, but Daniels thought that would hardly be likely out here on the flats. You could see trouble coming more than a mile off.

Guerrero was dressed like a vaquero, wearing chaps and a short leather jacket—even in this heat—and a wide-brimmed sombrero with fancy stitching around the base of its crown. The outfit made him stand out, because all of his companions, Curtis Daniels included, wore peasant clothing, the baggy light-colored pants and shirts of the farmers they had once been. Daniels had picked up a battered old sombrero during his travels, and his skin had been burned a dark brown by the sun since he had fled Texas. If not for his blond hair and tall, rangy build, he could have been mistaken for one of the Mexicans.

Might as well be a Mexican, he thought. He wouldn't ever be going back to Texas, not with a couple of murder charges hanging over his head.

His gaze turned northward for a moment, toward the border. The group was riding west, about halfway between El Paso and Chihuahua. His place had been down the Rio Bravo a ways from El Paso, about ten miles on the other side of the line. A few days' ride could have taken him back there . . . if there had been anything waiting for him but trouble and grief.

Guerrero had noticed him glancing off toward home. The man's lean, dark face creased in a grin. "Thinking about Texas, amigo?" he asked.

Daniels shrugged. "Don't know that I was thinking about anything. That takes too much work."

"I understand if you miss your home. Sometimes I wish I was a boy back in Monterrey. But those days are gone. That thrice-damned Frenchman and his Austrian lapdog have seen to that."

A grin tugged at the Texan's mouth, and he tipped his head down so that Guerrero wouldn't see it. He had been listening to Guerrero cuss Napoléon III and Maximilian for six months now, but despite his interest in politics, Guerrero had shown no signs of being anxious to join Juárez's revolution. He was too busy being a bandit.

"Reckon I'll stay right where I am," Daniels said

slowly. "No reason to go back to Texas."

"That is wise, amigo. You have found a new home here with us, this brave band of brothers, is this not so?"

"That's right, Ignacio. That's right."

Besides, if I did try to run out on you, you'd plug me in the back, Daniels continued silently. He knew what kind of man Guerrero was. You were either with him or against him, and if you were against him, he'd prefer you to be dead at the same time.

Daniels cast his mind back to the day six months or so earlier when he had first met Ignacio Guerrero. He had been exhausted from long hours on the trail, his throat bone-dry from the dust. And his mind was still as blasted by shock and sorrow as his body had been by the heat. He had gone into a cantina in a little settlement, looking for some shade and something to cut the thirst that was choking him. Instead he had found three bored *bandidos* who had decided it would be fun to rob and kill a foolish gringo.

He was pounding the skull of the third one into pulp against the hard-packed dirt floor of the place when Guerrero swaggered in, followed by a half-dozen of his men. Guerrero had paused just inside the cantina, blinking for second in surprise as he looked around. His quick gaze took in the overturned tables, the bartender cowering behind the rough bar, the two corpses—one with a bullet hole in his chest, the other with his head twisted at a strange angle on his neck—and the blond American who was sitting on top of the third dead man.

Daniels had looked up, met Guerrero's dark eyes, and in that instant believed he was about to die. His pistol was a good ten feet away, much too far. There was a knife sheathed at his back, but the edge was dull and he'd never been much of a hand with a blade to start with. The stranger in the vaquero outfit was wearing a Colt, and the men with him all had rifles. Nope, Daniels had thought, there was no way out. He was about to get shot to doll rags, and at the moment, he would have almost welcomed such a fate. Dying quick was about all a man like him could hope for.

Then Guerrero had thrown back his head and laughed.

"A veritable Samson, my friends, that is what we have here," he had said, Daniels easily following the Mex lingo. "He could not have done more damage had he been armed with the jawbone of an ass."

Daniels vaguely knew what the man was talking about, remembering some of the stories he'd heard preachers talking about back in east Texas, before he'd come west. He frowned, looked down at the dead man underneath him, and unlocked his fingers from around the corpse's neck. Without standing up, he indicated the other bodies and asked, "Friends of yours, mister?"

Guerrero had laughed again and shaken his head. "Friends of mine would not be so unwise as to waylay a man such as yourself, gringo. These men—and it unjustly honors them to name them so—are strangers to me." He strode across the floor and extended a hand to Daniels to help him up. "My name is Ignacio Guerrero, and I am pleased to make your acquaintance, sir."

Daniels had hesitated for a heartbeat, then taken Guerrero's hand.

That had been the start of it. Might have been better, he figured now, if Guerrero had just shot him instead. Daniels was coming to the conclusion that he wasn't cut out to be a bandit. It wasn't that he minded robbing from rich folks so much; he figured they could spare the money. But Guerrero had a habit of holding up whoever the gang came across, rich or poor, and he was quick to kill anyone who gave him any trouble. Daniels himself had not had to shoot anybody since that dustup in the cantina, but he had seen Guerrero and the other members of the bunch cut down quite a few men.

They were getting low on money and supplies again. Soon, Guerrero would be pulling another raid. Folks would probably die.

Maybe, Daniels thought, he would be one of them. If he was lucky . . .

"If my memory is correct, there is a rancho up ahead a few miles," Guerrero said suddenly. "The owner runs a cantina, as well. There will be provisions there and money for the taking." The outlaw's grin turned into a leer. "And maybe women as well, eh, amigo?" He slapped Daniels on the shoulder.

Daniels tried but couldn't summon up a smile. He said nothing, prompting Guerrero to frown suddenly and study him through slitted eyes. Then the Mexican shrugged expressively and looked ahead again.

He was probably thinking that all gringos were crazy, Daniels mused. Well, maybe that was the case. If he was so anxious to die, Guerrero would be glad to oblige him. All Daniels would have to do would be to cross him.

The Texan took a deep breath. He supposed that deep down, some damn fool part of him wasn't ready to die just yet after all. . . .

ONE

THE HUGE, BEARDED MAN stared into his glass of tequila for a moment, then tossed it down his throat. As the fiery stuff burned into his gut, he sighed in appreciation and settled back, the chair creaking dangerously under his massive form. The man let one long arm dangle near the bag of gold at his feet. Lying on top of the bag was an opossum, an ugly round animal with coarse gray fur and a long naked tail. It twisted its small head around, bared its sharp teeth, and hissed as the man's fingers scratched its back. The man silenced the creature with a glare and a rumbled, "Shut up, Stink."

Buffalo Newcomb sighed. Life was good.

He still had most of the five thousand dollars he had left El Paso with a few months earlier. He'd come out of that scrape with no wounds and five grand to the good, one of the better payoffs of his life. It could have been a lot more, but there was no use worrying about that now. Since crossing the Rio Bravo, he'd been drifting, visiting some señoritas he'd known in times past, catching up with other old friends at the same time.

Like Luis Vasquez. At the moment, the man was behind the bar of the cantina, bustling back and forth even though the place was not very busy in the middle of the day. There were only a handful of customers besides

Buffalo. Several vaqueros stood at the bar, drinking beer. Only one other table was occupied. Two men sat at it, both of them well-dressed, with faintly offended looks on their faces as if they thought it disgraceful that two such gentlemen should be forced to drink in a small cantina like this. There was a strong resemblance between them, and Buffalo had them figured for father and son. The girl with them, who was mighty good-looking from what he could see behind the veil over her face, was either the daughter of the older man or the wife of the younger one.

Buffalo had seen their carriage pull up outside, had noted the fine-looking animals in the team and the way the driver stayed respectfully outside after helping the three fancy ones alight from the vehicle. They were landowners, Buffalo had decided quickly, wealthy conservatives who supported the emperor Maximilian. Their business had to be pretty pressing to bring them out into the middle of nowhere like this, where you never knew when you might run into a band of Juárez's revolutionaries.

Luis Vasquez came out from behind the bar and over to Buffalo's table, pulling back a chair and settling down into it. He smiled across the table at the big man and lifted the glass he had brought with him. "To your health, my amigo," he said.

"And to wealth," Buffalo replied. "Without which, the first don't amount to a whole hell of a lot."

Vasquez sipped his tequila. "Ah, that is where you are wrong, my mercenary friend. Wealth means nothing without the warmth of home and family."

"Reckon you should tell that to them," Buffalo said, inclining his shaggy head toward the three people at the other table. "They look to me like they're a long way from home."

Vasquez glanced at them, and his round face wrinkled in a look of distaste as he looked back at Buffalo. "They ought to go back to Mexico City," he said in a low voice. "That kind sometimes brings trouble."

"You know 'em?"

"The old man is Don Hortensio Alvarez. He owns a great estate in Mexico City and has holdings all through the northern states. No doubt he has come to check on them, to make sure that his employees are not cheating him of the slightest peso. The boy is his son, Don Antonio." Vasquez shook his head, and there was contempt in his voice as he added, "They are landowners."

"So are you," Buffalo pointed out.

Vasquez shrugged. "It is different. I am a small rancher. I work for my rewards, both on my land and in this cantina. My family works. We do not rely on the blood and sweat of others for what we have. This is why the *Juaristas* do not bother us."

Buffalo was looking at the girl. "What about her?"

"Don Hortensio's wife."

"Don Antonio's, you mean."

"I mean what I say, my friend. The girl is wed to Don Hortensio."

A grin cracked Buffalo's bearded, leathery face. "The old goat," he chuckled.

Of course, Vasquez didn't do so bad himself, Buffalo thought. Working behind the bar now was his wife, Carlota, and she was a mighty handsome woman. There might be a few strands of gray in the mostly raven-black hair, and her waist might be a little thicker now, but she was still beautiful. And her tongue was sharp enough to damn near draw blood from anybody foolish enough to bring up the fact that she had the same name as that European trollop down in Mexico City who was calling herself an empress.

If anything, Carlota's daughter, Angelina, was even more beautiful than her mother. Vasquez didn't let Angelina work here in the cantina very often, and Buffalo could understand why. The girl's long, black hair and big, dark eyes would just about drive the vaqueros crazy if she were around much. That would lead to fights, and Vasquez ran a peaceful place.

Angelina was here at the moment, though, standing

behind the bar and talking to her mother in a low voice. From time to time, she cast a bashful glance at the table where Buffalo and her father were sitting. Buffalo had known her almost from the time she was a baby, which meant she probably figured he was like a disreputable old uncle. Damn shame, he thought. She was mighty pretty. But he'd keep his distance, out of respect for her mother and father.

Vasquez sighed. "I should bring in another barrel of tequila," he said, "but it is not often I get a chance to sit down with an old friend like this in the middle of the day. Will you be staying long?"

Buffalo shook his head in regret. "Just passin' through. Don't rightly know where I'm goin', but I ain't got the urge to light an' sit very long just yet. Figure I'll know when the time comes."

"I understand," Vasquez nodded. "You always were a wanderer, amigo. But it is good to see you and Señor Stink again."

Buffalo glowered down at the opossum. "Can't seem to get shed of the damn thing. Possums are stubborn critters. Foller a man from hell t' breakfast."

The Mexican grinned, not fooled for a second by Buffalo's gruff words. He said, "You will stay for supper at least?"

"Sure. And I wouldn't mind beddin' down in one of your barns tonight, neither. Looks like it might be cloudin' up to storm after while, and I never have been too fond of sleepin' in the rain."

"You will be most welcome, as always."

At the other table, Don Hortensio Alvarez looked up and spoke sharply. "Woman!" he said to Carlota. "More tequila."

Vasquez's mouth tightened as he heard the man's arrogant tone of voice. Buffalo saw the reaction and said softly, "Take it easy, pard. Reckon there's some of Maximilian's soldiers close by, otherwise them rich folks wouldn't be out here in such lonesome country."

"They did have an escort. I learned that much from

talking to the driver when I took him some water. But a band of *Juaristas* were spotted several miles east of here yesterday. The French captain decided to go chase them, rather than staying with Don Hortensio and his party. That is why the don came here. He was furious at the captain's decision, but he figured that they would be safe enough until the soldiers come back. I do not like it, but . . .'' Again, Vasquez shrugged.

The sound of hoofbeats drifted in from outside, carried on the hot air. Buffalo said, ''Maybe that's the soldier boys now.''

A few moments later, as the tall form of a man in a sombrero filled the doorway, silhouetted starkly against the bright afternoon sunlight, Buffalo knew he had been wrong. The man sauntered across the room to the bar, followed by five other men. His companions were wearing peasant clothes, but each man also carried a single-shot rifle, which made them look considerably more dangerous than the farmers they had appeared to be at first glance. Buffalo's eyes, hooded by heavy brows, darted from weapon to weapon, noting the condition the rifles were in and assessing the potential threat.

Carlota Vasquez had already emerged from behind the bar, bringing another bottle of tequila to the table where Don Hortensio and his wife and son sat. That left Angelina behind the bar alone, and Buffalo could see the grin on the face of the stranger as he greeted her. ''Hello, pretty one,'' the man said. ''Beer for me and my friends.''

Angelina nodded, keeping her eyes shyly downcast. She reached under the bar for a couple of buckets which she began to fill with beer from a cask. The other men crowded up to the bar, talking among themselves, and the coarse remarks a couple of them made were plainly audible to the girl. She blushed furiously and tried to ignore them.

The comments reached the table where Buffalo and Vasquez sat, too. Vasquez stiffened and started to push his chair back. Buffalo leaned forward, not seeming to move very fast, but his hand closed over Vasquez's arm before the cantina owner could stand up.

"Hold on," Buffalo hissed.

Vasquez turned an angry face toward him. "But you heard what they said about Angelina!"

"I heard," Buffalo agreed. "But I heard more'n that. There was at least a dozen horses in the bunch that just rode up. Where's the other six fellers?"

Vasquez frowned. He had lived on the Mexican frontier long enough to know when real trouble was about to bust wide open. If six men had stayed outside the cantina, there had to be a reason for it.

Carlota had hurriedly deposited the bottle of tequila on Don Hortensio's table, drawing looks of disapproval from the don and his son. She was stalking back behind the bar now, coming down the length of it so that she could stand beside Angelina and glower across the scarred wooden surface at the newcomers.

"This is a respectable cantina, señor," she said tartly. "Please mind your manners."

The vaquero lifted his hands in mock surprise. "But I have done nothing to offend, señora."

"Your friends have," Carlota shot back. "You should speak to them."

"Of course." The vaquero glanced around, his eyes lingering on Don Hortensio, Don Antonio, and the veiled girl. Interest sparked in his gaze.

More than interest, Buffalo thought. It was downright greed he saw in the man's dark eyes.

This was shaping up to be a damn sticky situation. Buffalo wondered for a few seconds what would happen if he got up and walked out of the place. Would the vaquero let him get on his mule and ride away? Could be the man would be happy to have Buffalo gone before he made his move.

Nope, Buffalo thought disgustedly. The vaquero's sharp eyes would never miss that heavy bag of gold, and Buffalo sure as hell wasn't going to leave without it.

Besides, he told himself as he sighed deeply, Luis

Vasquez and his family were his friends, and he didn't have so many of those that he could afford to run out on them.

The vaquero was still grinning as he said to his companions, "Watch what you say, my friends. We do not want to trouble these good people." His hand started to move toward the gun on his hip. "No, we do not wish to offend them. Only to rob them."

Then the gun was out, lined on the table where Don Hortensio sat. The other bandits snapped their rifles into position, covering everyone else in the cantina. Angelina gasped and cowered against the firm figure of her mother, who put one arm around the girl as she glared at the holdup men.

"What is the meaning of this?" Don Hortensio demanded, his white, spadelike beard quivering with indignation. "How dare you point that weapon at me?"

"I dare because I am Ignacio Guerrero, you old fool," the vaquero snapped, losing his grin. "And I will kill you if you cross me."

Don Antonio, his dark face now sallow with fear, was tugging at his father's sleeve as Don Hortensio stood up slowly. Don Hortensio ignored his son and faced Guerrero. "I will have you hunted down and shot for this outrage," the don said harshly.

"I think not," Guerrero said, and Buffalo could almost see his thumb start to lift from the drawn-back hammer of his Colt.

Suddenly, Luis Vasquez was on his feet, holding his empty palms toward Guerrero and saying quickly, "Please, señor! Take what you must, but do not harm anyone. We are peaceful people here. We want no bloodshed."

Guerrero managed to hold off and keep from firing. He glanced toward Vasquez and asked, "You run this place?"

"Sí. I am Luis Vasquez. This is my ranch, my cantina."

"Then you can tell me where you keep your money

and your provisions. We will take what you have but leave you with your lives if you do not resist." Without looking around, Guerrero inclined his head toward the bar. "I want the girl, too, the pretty young one. The old one you can keep."

Vasquez stiffened but said nothing. Buffalo knew good and well that Vasquez was not going to let the robbers ride away with Angelina as their prisoner. But the time wasn't right yet to make a move. . . .

Don Hortensio Alvarez was still on his feet. "This is impossible!" he said. "You filthy *Juaristas* think you can ride in and take anything you want."

Guerrero turned his attention back to the don. "We are not *Juaristas*, but the rest of what you say is right, old man. And I want *your* woman, too."

The girl in the veil shrank back against Don Antonio, who looked as if he wanted to be sick all over the floor. Buffalo glanced around the room. The vaqueros who had been drinking at the bar were all standing uneasily in a group, under the guns of the *bandidos*. None of the cowboys were armed, and when the showdown came, they wouldn't be much help. But maybe they could at least get in the way and distract some of Guerrero's men. The odds were still bad—especially when you considered the six missing riders.

Buffalo saw a flicker of movement at one of the windows and knew that the other six weren't missing anymore. They were doubtless waiting outside, rifles lined and ready to cut down anybody that the men inside missed.

There was a First Model Dragoon Colt holstered on Buffalo's hip underneath the filthy red poncho he wore. His Sharps was on the floor to his left, on the other side from the bag of gold. Sheathed on his right calf, the buttpiece just peeking from the fringed top of his boot, was the Arkansas Toothpick. He was sure he could take down a good four or five of the men before they killed him. But he'd still wind up dead.

A man couldn't go down without a fight, though. Vasquez was blocking Guerrero's view of him. Buffalo's right hand slid closer to the butt of the Dragoon.

Guerrero came nearer Don Hortensio's table, still menacing the landowner with his pistol. Don Hortensio did not give ground, standing stubbornly with his back ramrod stiff. Guerrero strolled to the other side of the table and reached out with his free hand to grasp the girl's veil. She sobbed as he ripped it away from her face, revealing lovely features. Maybe not quite as pretty as Angelina, Buffalo thought fleetingly, but damn near.

"Ah, yes," Guerrero said. "The girl definitely goes with me, old man. Your daughter?"

"My wife," Don Hortensio replied. "And I would sooner see her dead than being pawed by a dog like you."

Guerrero shrugged. "As you wish." The barrel of his pistol tilted toward the horrified girl.

Buffalo was moving, but surprisingly, Don Antonio beat him to it. The young don overcame his fear long enough to throw himself out of his chair and grab Guerrero's arm. Frantically, he twisted it aside as the bandit pulled the trigger and dropped the hammer.

The Colt blasted, the bullet driving into Don Antonio's midsection. A look of surprise flashed onto his face, as if things had not gone at all the way he had expected, and then he dropped away, releasing his grip on Guerrero's arm to clutch at his stomach.

Buffalo yelled, "Luis!" as he surged out of his chair. His left hand scooped the Sharps from the floor as he came up. He tossed the rifle toward Vasquez as the cantina owner whirled around.

At the same time, Buffalo's big right hand closed over the walnut grips of the Dragoon and swept it out of its holster. He was firing the instant that the barrel came level, the roar of black powder filling the room. Out of the corner of his eye, he saw Carlota and Angelina diving behind the bar for cover.

Vasquez caught the Sharps in midair and smoothly continued his turn, suddenly looking a lot more dangerous than the inoffensive little man that he had seemed. He brought the big rifle to his shoulder and fired, the blast even louder than the thunder of Buffalo's Colt. The slug tore through two of the bandits, spilling them to the floor.

An instant later, though, a bullet thudded into Vasquez's chest, staggering him. The Sharps slid from his hands as more lead tore into his body. Despite his courage, an agonized cry came from his lips as he stumbled forward.

Buffalo had squeezed off three shots and downed a couple of the robbers, but Guerrero was untouched so far. The bandit chieftain grabbed the girl and jerked her out of her chair, pulling her in front of him to use as a shield. Don Hortensio clawed futilely at Guerrero's jacket. Guerrero turned slightly and lashed out at the old man. The barrel of his pistol smashed into Don Hortensio's skull. Buffalo saw it hit, and even though he couldn't hear the crunching of bone over the storm of gunfire, he knew the landowner was done for.

The guns of the men outside started to bark as Buffalo threw himself to the side. The vaqueros who had been in the cantina to start with were getting into the fight now, knowing that they would probably die but selling their lives as dearly as possible. The men who had come in with Guerrero had burned their powder already and didn't have time to reload. The fighting was hand to hand now, fists against rifle butts and knives.

Buffalo squeezed off his last two shots, grimacing and cursing as only one bandit went down. He jammed the Dragoon back in its holster and bent to yank the big knife out of its sheath. In the same motion, his left hand closed around the tail of the possum, which had been scurrying frantically around his feet during the fight.

Several men were charging him, rifles lifted to use as clubs. As Buffalo straightened, his left arm whipped out. He let go of Stink's tail, and the writhing possum flew several feet through the air to crash into the face of one of the onrushing men. Claws dug in instinctively and

sharp teeth flashed as the animal bit at the man's nose
and eyes. He screamed in mortal terror, dropped his rifle,
and staggered backward, pawing at the creature attached
to his face.

Buffalo met the charge of the other men, slashing at
them with the Arkansas Toothpick. One of the bandits
fell back with blood fountaining from his throat. A rifle
butt slammed into Buffalo's right shoulder, numbing the
arm. He stabbed out again with the knife, driving a man
back. The arm refused to work right, though, and Buffalo staggered as another rifle butt drove into his side.

He looked up into the face of the man who had struck
the last blow and was shocked to see frightened, pale
blue eyes staring into his. There was blond hair under
the bandit's sombrero. The man was an American! But
that didn't stop him from drawing back the rifle to strike
again.

Buffalo hit him first, crashing his left fist into the bandit's face. The blond man went down, out cold.

It took only a second for Buffalo to transfer the knife
to his left hand then. He grinned at the men still facing
him, now including the ones who had rushed in from
outside, and roared, "Come on, damn ya! This ain't no
cotillion, boys!"

He saw Luis Vasquez's body lying motionless on the
floor. His old friend was dead, Buffalo was sure of that.
There was no sign of Carlota or Angelina, which meant
they were probably still hiding behind the bar. Buffalo
hoped they might have a chance to slip out while the
rest of the gang was busy killing him. Guerrero was
standing to the side, Don Hortensio's wife still clutched
in his left arm. She was writhing slightly, but it was clear
she was too frightened to put up much resistance. Her
husband was just as dead as Luis Vasquez, and Don
Antonio was whimpering as he died slowly from the
belly wound.

Buffalo's grin widened as he saw Stink scuttle away
off into a corner. The varmint would probably be all

right, Buffalo thought. Possums had a knack for survival.

The American was still sprawled at Buffalo's feet, out cold. The bandits looked at their fallen comrade, then at Buffalo, hesitating before charging him again. Others of their group were scattered around the room, lying in various broken, bloody poses. They were joined in death by the local vaqueros, all of whom had been either shot, knifed, or clubbed to death. The peaceful cantina was now a charnel house.

And it wasn't over yet. As Guerrero shouted, "Kill the gringo, dammit!" the rest of the bandits surged forward. Buffalo had time to wonder fleetingly why Guerrero didn't just shoot him. Maybe the man's honor had been insulted by having half of his gang killed off. He might not want the man responsible for most of those deaths to die too quickly.

Then all Buffalo had time for was hacking at the men surrounding him, letting the Arkansas Toothpick bite deeply into flesh as they flailed at him with their rifles. His right arm still wouldn't work. Blades cut at him, but he ignored the stings.

He kicked one man in the groin and sent him staggering past into the corner. Buffalo promptly forgot about him as he tried to deal with the others, until a couple of frantic minutes later he heard a shout behind him. Darting a glance over his shoulder, he saw that the man had caught up the bag of gold. Not paying any attention to what was inside the bag, the bandit was intent on using it as a weapon. Buffalo flung up an arm as the man swung the heavy bag at his head.

He was too late to do any good. The weight slammed into his arm, brushing it aside, then crashed against his head. Buffalo felt himself falling to the floor as a garish redness swept over his eyes. He landed on something soft, and then the red turned to black.

He didn't even feel it as the bandits began to beat him to death.

T W O

It was the sound of the rain that convinced Buffalo he was still alive.

When feeling had first started to seep back into his body, he had figured he was in hell. That would explain the aches and pains. Satan's imps were stabbing him with their pitchforks. It couldn't rain in hell, could it? That would put the fires out.

He pried his eyes open and forced the muscles in his neck to work, lifting his head so that he could peer around him. Dim gray light came in through the door and windows of the cantina. It was late afternoon, he judged, and one of the area's rare thunderstorms was going on outside. Thunder rumbled and lightning flickered, making the interior of the adobe building brighter for an instant, and in that space of time, Buffalo saw the bodies littering the floor.

His vision was a little blurry. He blinked his eyes until it cleared. The next flash of lightning showed him the same grisly sight.

Whatever he had fallen on was still under him. Buffalo moved a hand and felt the coarse fabric of a shirt. One of the bandits, he supposed. Buffalo grunted as he heaved himself to hands and knees, then climbed to his feet. He tried to ignore the pain shooting through him and the dizziness that made his head feel mushy.

He stepped over the man he had been lying on and staggered toward the bar. There was a lantern on the shelf behind it and a packet of matches sat next to the lantern. The big man's blunt fingers fumbled with the matches, finally scratching one of the lucifers into life and holding the flame to the wick. A deceptively cheerful yellow glow rose and filled the room as the lantern was lit. Buffalo turned and set it on the bar. Wind from the storm whipped through the room, making the flame waver slightly, but it kept burning.

Buffalo moved to the door and the windows in turn, pulling closed the pieces of canvas that covered them. That helped cut down the wind and stopped so much rain from spattering in. Thunder was still booming every so often.

Somehow, a bottle of tequila had managed to survive the melee inside the cantina. Buffalo went behind the bar, lifted the bottle from the shelf, and pulled the cork with his teeth. He spat it out, then lifted the neck of the bottle to his mouth.

When he lowered it long seconds later, the level of liquid inside had been considerably reduced. The stuff burned into his belly, warming him some and dulling the pain a little.

He couldn't postpone it any longer. He went to Luis Vasquez's body, knelt beside it, and checked for a pulse. There was none, of course. The cantina owner was cold, dead for long hours. The same was true of the other men scattered around the room, bandit and vaquero alike. Don Hortensio Alvarez lay with his eyes open and his mouth gaping, an ugly dent in the side of his head where Guerrero had fractured his skull. Nearby, Don Antonio had finally escaped the tortures of being gutshot. His face was twisted in a permanent contortion of agony.

There was no sign of Don Hortensio's wife, or of Angelina and Carlota.

Buffalo frowned. Guerrero had said that they wouldn't take Carlota. His men must have prevailed on him to change his mind. Even though she was older, she was still a better-looking woman than nine out of ten around here.

He walked slowly across the earthen floor toward the bandit he had fallen on. The man's sombrero had come off, and Buffalo could see his blond hair. The American. The one he had knocked out . . .

Buffalo reached over and plucked the lantern from the bar, going closer to the blond man. He knelt, studying the bloodstains that had turned the bandit's white shirt crimson in many places. The feller sure enough *looked* dead, Buffalo thought. He put a couple of fingers to the man's neck.

There was a pulse.

Buffalo sat back on his heels and thought this over. His own clothes were pretty bloody, although the stains were less visible on the red poncho. His beard was matted with blood that had come from his battered mouth and nose. There were some painful places on his side that he hadn't checked yet, but he figured they were knife wounds.

It became clear to him what had happened. He had been lying on top of the blond man while the rest of the bandits pummeled and stabbed him, and when the frenzy had finally left them, they had figured he was dead. Anybody looking at the blond man and seeing all that blood might assume that he was a goner, too. But the blood, or at least most of it, was Buffalo's.

He grunted. He was a big man; he had plenty of blood to lose. Besides, he'd already replaced some of it with tequila, and that seemed to work just as well.

It was a little surprising that Guerrero had left without making sure he was dead. Something must have happened to spook him. The bandits had been in a hurry to leave, Buffalo figured. It was a stroke of luck.

For him. Not for Guerrero.

A thought occurred to Buffalo. He turned his head and looked at the table where he had been sitting. A groan escaped his lips. The wounds he had suffered hadn't provoked such a reaction, but what he saw now did.

"Not my damn gold, too . . ."

But of course the bag was gone. Someone had thought to look inside it after it had been used to strike him down.

Buffalo stood up and replaced the lantern on the bar. He took a quick mental inventory. His gun and knife and rifle were gone, not surprisingly. He had the clothes on his back, a ratty old black hat, a possum hiding somewhere, and—if he was lucky—a mule outside.

And a prisoner. He put his hands on his hips, looked at the other American sprawled on the floor, and shook his head. What the devil was he going to do with a bandit?

There were broken bottles lying all around. It would be simple enough to pick up a good-sized chunk of glass and slit the man's throat before he came to. That would be the smart thing to do. You got rid of your enemies when and where you could.

Unless they could come in handy. Buffalo's forehead creased in thought. The rain would wipe out Guerrero's tracks, but the blond man might know where the bandits had been heading before they stopped here. Buffalo intended to find Guerrero, get back as much of his gold as he could, and pay the *bandido* back for what had happened. The blond man might be able to help him do that.

Best to keep him alive for now, Buffalo decided. He found some rope behind the bar and tied the man's hands and feet.

The rain stopped while he was doing that, the downpour slacking off suddenly and then fading away completely. Storms didn't come along very often out here, and when they did, they didn't last long. When the blond man was bound securely, Buffalo went to the doorway and pushed back the canvas. The clouds overhead were breaking up in a hurry as the storm moved on, and shafts of reddish-gold light from the westering sun began to thrust through the grayness.

Buffalo heard a rustling behind him and turned quickly, then relaxed as he saw the sharp-nosed face peering around an overturned table. "Howdy, Stink. Decided it was time to come out of your hidey-hole?"

The possum hissed at him.

"Now don't go holdin' a grudge just 'cause I flang you in that feller's face. Seemed like the thing t' do at the time. 'Sides, I notice one of them dead *bandidos* don't have a nose. Figger you bit it off 'fore the feller caught a stray bullet." Buffalo pointed a finger at the creature. "So don't go sayin' I never gave you nothin'."

He turned around and watched from the doorway as the sun came out. The thirsty ground was already sucking up the water that had fallen from the sky. It wasn't long before you could hardly tell whether it had even rained or not.

Buffalo had been dreading the chore that awaited him. But it had to be done, and as soon as the puddles had dried up, he got started.

He found a shovel in a lean-to in back of the cantina. The digging went easily in the soft dirt. Still, Buffalo felt fresh wetness on his shirt before he was finished. Those wounds were going to have to be attended to. He wanted to get the burying done first, though.

He dug a grave for Luis Vasquez, then a bigger hole for Don Hortensio and Don Antonio. Two more even larger graves would hold the vaqueros, he figured. He hated to have to lay them to rest so haphazard-like, but he knew he was too done-in to dig individual graves for the whole bunch. When the digging was done, he tossed the shovel aside and started toward the ranch house, about a quarter of a mile away. He hoped he would be able to find something there he could wrap Vasquez's body in before putting it in the ground.

So far he had seen no sign of his mule, which was damned annoying. Guerrero must have taken it with him, too, as well as the horses that had pulled Don Hortensio's carriage. The fancy vehicle was sitting to one side, empty.

Vasquez's rancho consisted of the small adobe house where the family lived, a couple of sod barns, and some corrals. The pair of vaqueros who had helped Vasquez run the place were lying dead back there in the cantina. The house itself was simple, with a small courtyard just inside the front door.

Buffalo stopped in his tracks as he stepped inside the place. He uttered a heartfelt curse, then averted his eyes from what he saw lying on the ground.

Carlota had put up a fight. That much had been evident in his brief glance. But the bandits had torn her clothes off and had their way with her, either before or after one of them had put a bullet through her head. Nobody had ever accused Buffalo Newcomb of anything resembling propriety, but he had too much respect for the memory of the woman to look at her nakedness now.

He figured that Carlota and Angelina had made a run for the house and reached it just as the bandits caught up to them. They'd had their fun with Carlota, finished her off, then taken Angelina with them when they left.

Before going, the robbers had ransacked the house, too. It was a mess, furniture overturned and broken, supplies looted from the kitchen, pure wanton destruction everywhere you looked.

Buffalo found a couple of pieces of canvas in a storeroom, though, and he used one of them to wrap Carlota's body. Gently, he lifted her to his shoulder and carried her back to the cantina.

He would have to dig another grave.

Finally, the grim task was finished. Luis and Carlota were resting side by side, the graves marked with simple wooden crosses that Buffalo had made from some of the shattered chairs inside the cantina. Sun and wind and rain would take the markers sooner or later, and the mounds of earth would sink and blend in with the soil around them. But it was the best Buffalo could do. The two landowners, father and son, and the vaqueros who

had been in the wrong place at the wrong time were
buried as well.

That left the dead bandits. Buffalo considered leaving
them where they were, but then decided it would be
better to get them out of the cantina. There was a small
ditch behind the building. He dragged the corpses out
there and dumped them into the gash in the earth, leaving them uncovered. The buzzards would take care of
the remainder of the chore.

That left him alone with the possum and the unconscious American. He went into the cantina, drew a
bucket of beer from a cask that hadn't been bullet-
punctured, and then pulled off his poncho and shirt. Sure
enough, there were a couple of gashes in his side where
somebody had taken a knife to him. He took a long swig
of beer, then picked up the bottle of tequila, which was
still half-full. Tequila wasn't as good as plain whiskey
for cleaning wounds, but it would have to do.

When he was done, Buffalo tied together some rags
he found underneath the bar and bound up the wounds
as best he could. Then he slipped his shirt and poncho
on again, guzzled some more beer, and righted one of
the overturned chairs. He placed it a few feet away from
the blond man, who was out cold but still breathing, and
sat down to wait.

He could be a mighty patient man when he had to be.
Ignacio Guerrero was going to find that out.

The American was starting to snort and move around a
little by the time darkness fell. He didn't wake up,
though, and Buffalo started to wonder if he had really
hurt the man's head.

Buffalo figured the American's age at about twenty-
five. He was rangy and rawboned, lantern-jawed enough
that nobody would ever call him handsome. His hands
had calluses like a farmer's hands; Buffalo had noticed
that while he was tying him up. But the marks were
fading, as if it had been a while since the man had used
a hoe or a plow. His rifle was gone, taken by his former

companions, but there had been a George Todd .36 Navy revolver in a holster on his hip. The gun was fully loaded, and Buffalo had appropriated it first thing.

There was no telling how the man had come to be running with a gang of Mexican bandits. He probably had some sad story about his past, but Buffalo didn't care about hearing it. All he wanted to know was where he could find Guerrero.

Hunger was starting to gnaw at the big man's belly. He found some tortillas and a hunk of cheese behind the bar and ate them, washing them down with more beer. That helped a little, but between the blood he had lost, the digging he had done, and the beer and tequila he had poured down his throat, he was starting to feel a little light-headed.

Maybe he was downright drunk, he realized a few minutes later when he looked up and saw the little man standing in the doorway of the cantina, pointing a rifle at him.

"Mind pointin' that somewhere else, sonny?" he grunted. "It's liable to go off, the way you're shakin'."

"Silence!" the stranger snapped. He wore expensive, tight-fitting pants and jacket, and there was a felt sombrero atop his sleek, dark head. "Do not move, señor, or I will be forced to kill you. Who are you, and what are you doing here? Who is that man?"

"You told me to be quiet," Buffalo reminded him.

"Answer my questions!"

Buffalo took a deep breath. The stranger was around thirty years old, and clearly he was frightened almost out of the fancy pants he was wearing. Few things were more dangerous than a scared man with a gun. On the other hand, the barrel of the rifle was wavering around so much there was a good chance any shots would go wild and miss their target. Still, Buffalo's head was starting to hurt, and he didn't want any gunplay if it could be avoided. The noise could make his headache worse.

"Name's Buffalo Newcomb," he said. "I don't know this other feller's name."

"And how did you come to be here? Where is Luis Vasquez?"

"The grave's out back," Buffalo sighed. "Him and Carlota both are laid to rest out there."

The man's eyes got even wider. "Dead? Both of them? . . . *Dios* . . . What of Angelina?"

Buffalo shook his head. "Don't rightly know. I figger a bunch of bandits carried her off."

"Bandits?"

"Bunch led by a man named Ignacio Guerrero. They hit the place early this afternoon."

Sweat was running down the stranger's face. "I do not believe any of this!" he exclaimed. "You are to blame for this!"

"You're wrong, son," Buffalo said quietly. "Vasquez was my friend. I've got a couple of knife wounds in my side and a few lumps on my head to back up my story."

The young man put a sneer on his face and gestured with the rifle barrel at the American. "And I suppose this poor devil is one of the so-called bandits?"

"That's right."

"He is a gringo!"

"Maybe so," Buffalo shrugged. "He still tried to cave in my skull during the ruckus."

"Stand up and back away from him."

Buffalo sighed and did as he was told, retreating to the bar. The stranger came farther into the cantina, walking slowly toward the American. He kept his rifle pointed in Buffalo's general direction.

The stranger knelt as he reached the American, frowning as he glanced down to study the blond man's face. The captured bandit was stirring even more now, and his eyelids were beginning to flicker.

Holding the rifle with one hand and reaching behind him with the other, the stranger produced a small knife. Buffalo growled, "You ain't thinkin' about cuttin' him loose, are you?"

"That is exactly what I intend to do," the man

snapped. "I will get the truth from him. I expect I will discover that *you* are the bandit, señor, and that you are responsible for the deaths of my beloved cousins."

"Cousins?"

"*Sí*. I am Rafael Sebastiano y Roderigo Vasquez. The humble family that ran this cantina were my cousins."

He put the knife closer to the bound wrists of the American, ignoring Buffalo's glower. A moment of sawing with the sharp blade parted the slender rope.

"Dammit, get away from him!" Buffalo snapped. "Can't you see he's wakin' up?"

"Do not move!" Rafael Vasquez ordered as Buffalo took a step forward. "If you come any closer, I will shoot—"

The American's now-free left hand flashed up, closing over the barrel of Rafael's rifle and thrusting it to the side. At the same moment, he struck with his right, his fist crossing the Mexican's jaw in a blow that jerked Rafael's head around and sent him sprawling. The blond man started to roll, jerking the rifle out of Rafael's stunned grip.

"Oh, hell!" Buffalo Newcomb exclaimed, grabbing for the .36 revolver stuck behind his belt.

THREE

CURTIS DANIELS DIDN'T HAVE any idea what was going on, but he knew he wasn't among friends. That had been obvious as soon as he felt the cords binding his hands and feet.

But then the ropes on his wrists fell away suddenly, cut loose by somebody kneeling over him. Daniels had a glimpse of the man as he opened his eyes, and then he saw the rifle.

He had been captured, and now his captors were about to execute him as a bandit! That thought flashed through his mind, making his body start moving of its own volition.

He grabbed the rifle and hit the man looming over him, his stiff muscles protesting as he forced them to work. There were more twinges of pain as he rolled to the side, away from the Mexican. A voice roared, ''Hold it, boy!''

The room swam before Daniels's eyes. A heavy ache was thudding inside his head as he jerked the barrel of the rifle up and found the trigger guard with a fumbling finger. He blinked, trying to find a target. He was operating on instinct, determined to fight until the last breath in his body.

He heard footsteps, looked up to see a massive figure

looming over him. A booted foot kicked the rifle out of his hands. Daniels let out a cry of futile rage as the weapon went clattering away from him.

A hand caught his collar, and he felt himself lifted off the floor, seemingly effortlessly. Daniels stared for an instant into an ugly, bearded face and saw the anger in the man's eyes. Then he was being flung away to crash into a wall. His still-tied legs wouldn't hold up his weight, and he sank down into a sitting position, back against the wall, legs stuck out in front of him. His chest heaved as he tried to draw air into his lungs.

In front of him, the small Mexican who had cut his hands free leaped toward the big bearded man. It was like one of those little hairless dogs trying to herd a bull. The bearded man swatted the Mexican with the back of one paw and sent him spinning to the floor. Then he turned back to Daniels, leveled a pistol at him—his own .36 Navy!—and said, "Don't get any more hasty ideas, son. I'm gettin' a mite tired of folks tryin' to kill me."

Daniels sucked in a ragged breath. "Wh-who the hell . . . are you, mister?"

The bearded man frowned. "You don't recollect tryin' to stove in my skull with a rifle butt?"

Daniels closed his eyes and groaned. Memories of the fight in the cantina came flooding back to him. He recalled rushing this big gringo with the other members of Guerrero's band who had survived the initial fighting. The last thing he remembered was the man's huge fist about to crash into his face. After that there was nothing until just a couple of minutes earlier.

"I remember now," Daniels said with a sigh.

"Damn well should." The bearded man scowled at him, and it was a sight to curdle milk. "You an' your compadres tried to kill me, and I don't take kindly to that." He stared at Daniels over the barrel of the .36. "Give me one good reason I shouldn't ought to just blow your brains out right here an' now."

Daniels's eyesight was clearer now. He had no trouble seeing the menace in the big man's cold glare. Everything about the man said that he had killed plenty of times before and would not hesitate to kill again. But he had let Daniels live this long, and that had to mean something.

Taking a deep breath, Daniels said, "I ain't got one good reason, mister. But you must have, or you would have shot me or cut my throat before now."

He thought he saw a flicker of surprise in the big man's eyes. The barrel of the Todd lowered an inch or so. It was still plenty threatening, but at this point, Daniels was ready to take any kind of leeway he could get.

"That little nap must not've muddled your brain too much," the bearded man grunted. "You just sit there and don't do anything stupid, and you might live awhile longer." He turned to the Mexican, who was moaning and trying to pull himself into a sitting position. "Don't go carryin' on so! Hell, I didn't even knock you out. This feller was out cold for three or four hours."

That told Daniels a little more about his situation. And it explained why his head hurt so bad. As the bearded man bent over and hauled the Mexican to his feet, Daniels took his first good look at his new companions.

Even if he hadn't been so striking-looking, the big man would have dominated any room he was in by his sheer size. He topped six feet by an inch or two and must have weighed close to three hundred pounds. Some of it was fat—a considerably belly was only partially hidden by a filthy red poncho—but from the width of his shoulders and the legs like tree trunks encased in greasy pants, muscle accounted for plenty of his weight. There was a buffalo design on the poncho, but Daniels was no expert on Indians; he couldn't identify which tribe the garment might have come from originally. A battered black hat was shoved to the rear of the man's head, revealing a thatch of shaggy black hair liberally shot through with gray. The bushy beard was the same color. As the man turned his head slightly, Daniels could see both a jagged scar on his left cheek and a single short braid in the hair. What looked like a rattlesnake rattle was tied to the braid. The man was impressive, all right, and so was his scent. Daniels could smell him ten feet away.

The Mexican, on the other hand, was small and slender, and he looked even punier standing next to the big man, practically dangling from his hand. The earlier blow had knocked off his sombrero. It lay on the floor nearby, high-crowned and filigreed with silver threads, the hat of a rich man—or at least one who was trying to appear wealthy. There was no telling where it might have been stolen.

The rest of the Mexican's outfit seemed to go with the sombrero, however. The dark brown pants with fancy stitching, the short matching jacket, the frilly white shirt, the soft boots . . . These were all garments such as a dandy from Mexico City might wear.

"Now," the big man rumbled, shaking the Mexican, "are you goin' to listen to reason, Rafael whatever-your-name-is? I didn't kill nobody but some damn bandits, and if the Vasquezes was your cousins, then I'm right sorry I had to be the one to break the bad news to you. Now sit down and keep your trap shut!"

He all but threw the Mexican into a chair, then turned back to Daniels. "Name's Buffalo Newcomb," he grunted. "And you're right, son, I got a reason for keepin' you alive. I want Guerrero, want him bad."

Daniels nodded slowly. "I was starting to figure as much. And you think I can tell you where to find him."

Buffalo Newcomb grinned and let the barrel of the .36 line up with Daniels's head again. He said, "Better hope for your sake that you can."

"I . . . I don't reckon I know. I've only been riding with him for a few months, and we just sort of drifted around—"

"Robbin' and killin' folks," Buffalo finished when Daniels stopped abruptly.

Daniels took a deep breath. "I never killed anybody who wasn't trying to kill me."

The Mexican spoke up, saying quickly, "A thousand

pardons, Señor Buffalo. But would someone please tell me what happened here? I come to see my relatives for a peaceful visit, and now I . . . I am devastated to find that they are dead.''

"I told you what happened," Buffalo said, without taking his eyes off Daniels. "A bunch of *bandidos*, includin' this feller, rode in whilst I was here visitin' and tried to hold up the place. If that was all they'd done, might be nobody would've got shot. But the head man was bound and determined to kidnap your cousin Angelina and another gal who happened to be here, and he started shootin' folks when the other gal's husband didn't cotton to the idea. After that, it got a mite hectic.'' To Daniels, he said, "That sound about the way it happened, farmer?''

Daniels started. "How'd you know I used to be a farmer?''

Buffalo gestured with the pistol. "Could tell it by your hands. And you sure as hell ain't much of a *bandido*.''

There was no reason he should be offended by such a comment, especially under the circumstances, but Daniels found himself flushing angrily.

To the Mexican, Buffalo went on, "After the farm boy got hisself knocked out, I waltzed around with his pards for a while 'fore one of 'em coldcocked me with somethin' he shouldn't have. Ain't rightly sure what went on after that, but I woke up here, and this feller and me was the only ones still alive.''

"Daniels. My name is Curtis Daniels.''

Buffalo shook his head. "I don't give a damn what your name is, son. You ain't no good to me less'n you know where Guerrero went, and I'd just as soon've shot you 'fore you told me who you are.''

"Well, it's too late now," Daniels said hurriedly, grasping for any chance at survival he might find. "You know my name now, Newcomb, and if you shoot me, you'll know that you're killing a fellow American. A fellow Texan, by the sound of you.''

"American, Mexican, that don't make no never mind to me." Buffalo started to lift his thumb from the hammer of the Todd.

"Wait a minute!" Daniels cried. "I may not know where Guerrero is now, but I know where he might've been headed."

"Thought you said y'all was just driftin'." Buffalo frowned, but he held off on firing.

"Yeah, but pickings had gotten slim. This war between the *Juaristas* and Maximilian has made everybody careful—and made a lot of people poor."

"Hard times for a bandit, you're sayin'."

Daniels nodded. "That's right. Guerrero had started talking about going back to this place he used to have in the mountains. Some sort of stronghold. I don't know where it is; that was before I rode with his band. But I bet we can find it."

" 'We'?" Buffalo echoed doubtfully.

Daniels leaned forward. His voice was sincere as he said, "Take me with you when you go after him, Newcomb. I've got a score to settle with the bastard myself. He left me here to die, didn't he?"

"I been wonderin' about that," Buffalo allowed. "He must not've had a very high opinion o' you, Daniels."

"I don't know. Like I said, I hadn't been riding with Guerrero for long."

The big man snorted in disgust. "And that's supposed to make me think I can trust you, feller? You done tried to kill me once today already. I ain't just about to let you ride behind me."

"I had to go after you. Guerrero would've shot anybody who didn't follow his orders, and we all knew it."

Buffalo reached behind him and picked up a corked bottle that still had a few inches of tequila in it. He tossed the bottle to Daniels, who plucked it deftly from the air despite his surprise.

"Reckon that sounds like somethin' Guerrero would do, all right," Buffalo said. "Ain't sure that I believe you, Daniels, and I may shoot you yet. But there ain't no reason you can't have a drink whilst we're sortin' this out.''

"Thanks," Daniels said gratefully, suddenly aware of just how dry his mouth really was. He uncorked the bottle and upended it, swigging the liquor and savoring its hot kick as it hit his belly. He drained the rest of the tequila and then wiped the back of his hand across his mouth.

The Mexican interjected himself in the conversation again. "I say we kill the gringo," he commented harshly. "He obviously knows nothing that will help us locate Angelina."

Buffalo frowned. "Nobody invited you along, either, Pancho. And I ain't said I'm goin' after those gals."

"But you must! If they are the captives of such a band of thieves, who knows what horrible fate is in store for them?"

"I know damn well," Buffalo replied, "and you do, too. Ain't nothin' we can do to stop that."

"You might be able to get them back alive, though," Daniels put in. "With my help, that is."

"And I will thank you to remember my proper name, Señor Buffalo. It is Rafael Sebastiano y Roderigo Vasquez."

"Dammit, who's got the gun here?" Buffalo exploded. "What gives you two varmints the right to tell me what to do?"

"You know we're right, Newcomb," Daniels said quietly. "You already told us you're going after Guerrero. What other reason could you have except to rescue those two girls?"

What might have been a shrewd look appeared on the big man's bearded face. "That ain't none o' your business, either of you. And even if I didn't have any other reason, I don't like to let folks get away with tryin' to kill me. Makes for bad talk about a man, happen he don't kill them what tries to kill him."

Daniels pointed at his ankles. "So untie my feet and let's scare up some mounts and go after Guerrero."

"Only kill the gringo first, Señor Buffalo," Rafael added.

Abruptly, Buffalo let the hammer down on the pistol and stuck it behind his felt again. "I ain't killin' nobody—yet. Rafael, pick up that little pigsticker you dropped a while ago and finish cuttin' Daniels loose."

"As you told me, señor, that is a mistake," Rafael warned.

"Just do what I tell you, blast it!"

Buffalo went behind the bar while Rafael came over to pick up his knife and sever the ropes around Daniels's ankles. The Mexican glared at Daniels and looked as if he wanted to plunge the blade into his heart, but he settled for saying under his breath, "If it was up to me . . ."

"But it's not, is it?" Daniels snapped, leaning over to try to rub some feeling back into his feet. Buffalo could tie a good, tight knot.

There was a thump as Buffalo set another bottle of tequila on the bar. "Reckon there ain't no end to miracles," he muttered. "Found another 'un that ain't shot up. Both you boys come over here and have a drink, and we'll study on what we're goin' to do."

Awkwardly, Daniels got to his feet and followed Rafael to the bar. His legs didn't want to work properly at first, and the pounding headache inside his skull made his balance wobbly. But he navigated across the cantina successfully and reached out to take the bottle when Buffalo extended it to him.

"Don't go to figgerin' I trust you, just 'cause I had Rafael turn you loose," Buffalo said darkly as he handed over the tequila. "You'll be ridin' in front of me the whole way, mister."

"Then you are going after Angelina?" Rafael asked.

"Told you I wanted to catch up to Guerrero. If them gals are still alive when we do, maybe we can get 'em loose."

Daniels swallowed some of the fiery liquor, then passed the bottle to Rafael. The little Mexican looked at

it with an expression of distaste, but after a second he
lifted it as well and drank.

"So you ain't got no idea where this hideout of Guerrero's is?" Buffalo said to Daniels.

"I don't know for sure. But I heard him talk about it
a few times. It's up high in the mountains somewhere,
but there's a valley close by, with a village and some
farms. Guerrero made it sound like a pretty place. A
good place to lick his wounds; he lost quite a few men
today."

"If it's in the mountains, that's west of here," Buffalo
mused. "We can start out in that direction, maybe pick
up his trail in a day or two. That rainstorm we had earlier
will've wiped out any tracks round here, but it was
movin' east." The big man nodded. "Yep, we should
be able to trail the bastard."

This was the first that Daniels had heard about any
rainstorm, but now that Buffalo mentioned it, he thought
the night air smelled a little different, a little cleaner and
fresher. Of course, it was hard to tell with the big man
so close by. . . .

"I know I'm goin' to hate myself for askin' this,"
Buffalo said, "but how'd you come to be ridin' with a
snake like Guerrero, Daniels?"

The rangy Texan shrugged. "Didn't have much
choice in the matter. It was either join up with the band
or get robbed and killed by them. I joined up. I've been
wishing ever since, though, that I'd never run into
them."

"Didn't take to the *bandido* life, huh?"

"I didn't like stealing from innocent folks," Daniels
said flatly. "And I sure as hell didn't like the way Guerrero gunned down anybody who got in his way."

"How come you didn't leave?"

"I guess I was a coward." He didn't flinch from saying it. "It was easier to just go along with what Guerrero
wanted. I didn't want to have to think about anything or
make any decisions. Anyway, where could I go?"

"Back across the border, to that farm I reckon you had."

Daniels shook his head. "I couldn't do that, either. The law in Texas wanted me. Still does, I suppose."

It all sounded pretty shameful, now that he had been forced to lay it out in words. He was a wanted criminal, a man on the run who had fallen in with a gang of murderers and thieves simply because it was the easiest thing to do. It was an ugly picture, all right.

Buffalo turned to Rafael. "What about you? How come you to ride in right after them bandits hit this place?"

"Sheer happenstance, I assure you, Señor Buffalo. I was on my way to visit my dear cousins—"

"By yourself?" Buffalo cut in. "Out here in the middle of nowhere?"

Rafael flushed. "I know what you are thinking. You believe that a man such as myself is soft and pampered and would not attempt such a journey. But I am stronger than I look, señors. I was a member of the army at one time. I can take care of myself."

Daniels wasn't convinced of that, but he didn't say anything. If he and Rafael were going to be allies of a sort, unwilling though the situation might be, it wouldn't help matters to insult the Mexican's pride.

Buffalo took the bottle, downed a healthy slug of the tequila. "All this talk about goin' after Guerrero don't take one thing into account—how're we goin' to chase him when we don't have but one horse?" He looked at Rafael. "You ain't got an extra couple of mounts with you, do you?"

Rafael shook his head. "No, I have only a pack mule and my own mount."

"Well, the mule'll do for me. Guess the two of you can double up on the horse."

The look Rafael gave Daniels made it clear how he felt about that suggestion, but he didn't say anything. Riding double would slow them down, too, but there was nothing that could be done about it.

"We'll go through the rancho and see if we can find some more guns," Buffalo went on. "I ain't overly fond of the idea of facin' Guerrero with just this here .36 Navy and that carbine of yours, Rafael. Maybe Guerrero's men overlooked somethin'. Seems like they left in a hurry, anyway."

"They must have," Daniels agreed. "Otherwise, Guerrero would have put a bullet through your head just to make sure you were done for."

"That's what I figgered." Buffalo offered the tequila to them again, and when Daniels and Rafael both shook their heads, he corked it and said, "Reckon we might as well round up that hoss and mule of yours, Rafael, and head up to the house. We can get a fresh start first thing in the mornin', and I ain't partial to the thought of stayin' here in the cantina overnight."

Daniels glanced around at the blood splattered on the floor and walls and repressed a shudder. He understood what Buffalo meant. He hadn't asked what the big man had done with the bodies that had been left behind when Guerrero and the rest of the band fled. He wasn't sure he wanted to know.

Buffalo reached under the bar and brought out an empty sack that had once held supplies of some sort. He muttered, "Hold on a minute, fellers," then stooped over again and scooped something up from the floor. Daniels's eyes widened as he saw the ugly gray animal dangling from Buffalo's hand. A surprised exclamation in Spanish came from Rafael.

"What's the matter?" Buffalo asked as he held the bag open with one hand and dumped the squirming animal into it. "Ain't you two never seen a possum before?"

"Not lately," Daniels said. "And I don't recollect ever seeing somebody carry one in a sack."

"Well, you have now. Come on."

Buffalo gestured for him to lead the way out of the place. Daniels was a little steadier on his feet now as he headed for the doorway. Buffalo waited until Rafael had

fallen in a couple of feet behind Daniels before he came
out from behind the bar. Daniels glanced back and saw
that Buffalo had his hand on the butt of the revolver,
taking no chances. Allies they might be, but the big man
was not going to put too much trust in either of his
companions.

Daniels stepped out into the night, heard an all too
familiar sound, and stopped short. Rafael bumped into
his back and cursed, and Buffalo snapped, "What the
hell you stoppin' for—"

"No one will go any farther," a voice commanded in
French-accented Spanish, "or my men will fire! Now,
you will please to raise your arms. You are all prisoners
of the Emperor, His Majesty Maximilian!"

"Dammit," Buffalo said fervently. "I knew I was
forgettin' somethin'."

F⬧O⬧U⬧R

THE MEXICAN SOLDIERS CAME out of the darkness surrounding the cantina, keeping their rifles trained on Buffalo, Daniels, and Rafael as they encircled the three men. In the light that came through the open doorway of the building, Daniels could see the disgusted look on Buffalo's face. One of the soldiers darted forward, snatched the pistol from the big man's belt, and hurried back to his place.

A man in a more elaborate uniform managed to swagger as he emerged from his place of concealment behind a mesquite. He paused before he got too close, staying well out of reach as he faced them. "So," he said, his accent revealing him to be the same man who had called out to them, "are you *Juaristas* or merely bandits?"

"Neither one, Cap'n," Buffalo replied. "We're just poor honest citizens who're passin' through these parts."

The officer shook his head. "Do not attempt to fool Captain Henri Reynard, m'sieu. I know a law-abiding man when I see one, and you, sir, are not of that breed." His expression became more taut and worried. "Where are Don Hortensio Alvarez and Don Antonio Alvarez?"

"If you're talkin' about a couple of fancy-dressed

fellers who looked like they might've been father and son, they're buried out back.''

Reynard's eyes narrowed in shock. "And what about Doña Isabella?''

"Don't reckon I know," Buffalo said with a shrug of his massive shoulders. "Didn't even know there was a gal here 'til you just said so.''

Daniels frowned. That was an outright lie. Buffalo knew perfectly well of the existance of Don Hortensio's wife. It seemed logical enough under the circumstances for the big man to tell this Captain Reynard about Guerrero's raid and enlist his help in chasing down the band of renegades. Daniels hoped Buffalo wouldn't do that, though.

Reynard looked skeptical, as well he should have. He said, "Are you telling me that you three men are not members of the gang we chased away from here late this afternoon?''

"Like I told you, mister," Buffalo insisted, "we're just innocent travelers who rode in here and found a bunch of people shot up.''

The captain gestured at the bag Buffalo was holding. It was still now, the possum having settled down. "And what is that?'' Reynard demanded. "Are you stealing from the dead?''

Buffalo glowered at that suggestion, but he kept his temper under control as he said, "This here's just a pet of mine.''

"Oh, I am certain of that, m'sieu," Reynard said, his contemptuous tone of voice making it clear that he was not at all certain of it. "Please hand the bag over and allow me to inspect this so-called pet of yours.''

"Well . . . if you reckon you should.'' Buffalo thrust the bag toward Reynard, and the movement made Stink start to squirm again.

The French officer took the bag and jerked the drawstring top open, peering into its interior in the dim light. Suddenly, he jerked back and let out a shout as the possum's sharp-toothed snout darted out of the bag. Reynard dropped it, but Buffalo's deceptive speed allowed him to catch the bag before it hit the ground.

"It's a possum," Buffalo said dryly. "Don't rightly know why I keep him. He smells bad, and he ain't very friendly."

Daniels thought that was a pretty good description of Buffalo himself.

Reynard held himself with the stiffness of embarrassment and said, "I will thank you to keep that animal under control, m'sieu. If you allow it to run loose in the camp, I shall issue orders that it is to be shot."

"Don't worry. I'll keep ol' Stink right with me."

From the angry look on Reynard's face, Daniels thought it might be a good time to change the subject. He spoke up for the first time, nervous because of the guns pointed at him but wanting to find out more about what had happened that afternoon. "You say you chased a gang away from here?" he asked the captain.

"*Oui*. As we were returning to the cantina, our scouts spotted the dust from several men leaving this place in a hurry. Thinking that there might be trouble, we pursued them." Reynard frowned at him. "But I have answered enough questions, m'sieu. I must insist that you answer mine."

Well, that explained why Guerrero had taken off in such a hurry, Daniels thought. He or one of his men had spotted the troops approaching in time for the gang to light out from the cantina. And obviously, Reynard had not had his wits about him enough to send anyone to the cantina to see what had happened. He had taken all of his troops and pursued the fleeing robbers, probably thinking how Maximilian would reward him if he wiped out a band of *Juaristas*.

It was clear that Guerrero had given the soldiers the slip, and now Reynard had come back to the cantina to see what he could find out. Buffalo didn't seem inclined to cooperate, though.

Daniels still didn't understand that, but he wasn't going to argue with the big man's decision. As a member—former member?—of Guerrero's bunch himself, he would be facing a firing squad or a lynch rope if the officer found out the truth about him.

"I'm sorry, Captain," he said, after a moment in which those thoughts crowded through his head. "I don't know any more about it than my friend here has already told you."

Reynard sighed in exasperation and turned to Rafael. "What about you? Are you going to be as stubborn about it as these two gringos?"

Rafael shrugged expressively. "I can only tell you what I know, Captain. Which is nothing."

That surprised Daniels a little. He had halfway expected the little dandy to spill everything. From the look on Rafael's face, though, he had little love for the French officers whom Maximilian had placed in command of the Mexican army. Daniels recalled Rafael saying that he had been in the army; maybe he had lost his own position to a French interloper.

Reynard glared at the three of them. "I could have you shot, you know," he threatened. "You and your . . . possum." Distaste dripped from his voice.

Daniels looked at Buffalo, saw the stolid expression on his face. "Reckon you'll have to shoot us, then," Buffalo said. " 'Cause we can't tell you a damn thing."

Reynard spent several seconds cursing in French, then switched back to Spanish and told his troops, "We will camp here tonight. I want these men tied up and placed in a tent until I decide what to do with them."

Under the threat of the muskets pointing at them, Buffalo, Daniels, and Rafael stood and allowed their hands to be lashed behind their backs. Then they were prodded away from the cantina as several of the soldiers began pitching tents in a line, several yards away from the cantina.

Reynard took a detail and went behind the building. When he returned a little later, it was obvious from the sick, washed-out look on his face that he had found the bodies of the dead *bandidos* in the ditch. Daniels wished that he wasn't wearing the same sort of clothes as the dead men. Still, it was common enough garb here south of the border. Reynard might not take it to mean that he was a member of the same gang.

They had not been placed in one of the tents yet. Reynard stalked over to them and snapped, "You say Don Hortensio and his son are buried out there?"

"That's right," Buffalo rumbled. "That is, if the fellers you're talkin' about was wearing fancy getups like grandees. We put 'em in the same hole to save some diggin'. Same with some vaqueros we found inside the cantina. The man and woman who looked like they might've run the place, them we buried side by side." He spat. "Tossed them dead bandits in the ditch."

"How do you know they were bandits?" Reynard asked sharply.

"Hell, it figgers, don't it?" Buffalo put a sheepish smile on his face. "Reckon you spooked us when you come up out'n the dark that way, cap'n. That's the only reason we got muley and wouldn't talk to you. Way we had it figgered, a bunch of bandits hit this place earlier today. That had to've been them you chased off. My pards an' me come along later and stumbled in on a mighty ugly sight, yes, sir. All them dead bodies was enough to make any man skittish."

Reynard nodded slowly. "Of course. And I am glad that you have decided not to be so stubborn, m'sieu. Now, if I could have your names."

"Sure thing. I'm Jupiter Smith, this here's George Duncan, and our dark-skinned pard there is Pancho Garcia."

Rafael glowered, but he made no move to contradict what Buffalo was saying to Reynard. Daniels kept his mouth shut, too. He had no idea what Buffalo was up to. This game had gotten too deep for him in a hurry.

"Very well, M'sieu Smith. I appreciate your cooperation."

"Then how about untyin' us?" Buffalo asked.

Reynard snapped his fingers at a nearby soldier. "It

shall be done.'' As the Mexican trooper moved in to free them, Reynard went on, ''Might I ask what the three of you are doing in this vicinity, sir?''

''Prospectin'. Or rather, headin' for the Sierra Madre to do some prospectin'. Hear tell there's gold up there, if you can sniff it out and then keep the Apaches from takin' your hair.''

''Indeed. The Apaches do present a problem from time to time. Between them and the *Juaristas*, this part of Mexico is not safe for its own citizens, let alone visitors. It might be wise for you and your friends to return to wherever you came from, M'sieu Smith.''

''Sounds like good advice, cap'n. I reckon that's just what we'll do.'' With his hands freed now, Buffalo rubbed his wrists to get the circulation going again. Daniels and Rafael were doing the same thing. ''Reckon we could camp here with you fellers tonight? With bandits around, I don't much want to be out by ourselves.''

''Certainly. I understand. In the morning, however, we will be heading west to try to pick up the trail of the criminals again. I expect you and your companions to go east.''

Buffalo nodded in agreement. ''We'll sure do 'er, cap'n.''

Reynard waved a hand at the tent they were standing in front of. ''You might as well use this tent,'' he offered. ''But stay close to it. There will be sentries out, and you might accidentally be shot if you wander too far.''

''We'll remember that, won't we, boys?'' Buffalo asked, and Daniels and Rafael nodded.

Reynard inclined his head in dismissal, then sauntered off to see to the rest of the setting up of camp. Buffalo plucked back the canvas over the opening of the tent and gestured curtly for the other two to go inside. He followed, letting the canvas flap drop shut behind him.

The little tent was too full with Buffalo inside it. Daniels felt like he couldn't get his breath, and Rafael seemed to be affected the same way. A little light came in through the gaps around the entrance, a reddish-yellow glow cast by the campfire that Reynard had ordered built.

"Damn fool'll have *Juaristas*, bandits, and Apaches down on his head 'fore mornin', showin' that much light," Buffalo muttered. "I'm glad we won't be here."

"Where are we going?" Rafael demanded. "And what in the name of God was that all about, Señor Buffalo? Pancho Garcia? *Dios mio!*"

"That was all I could think of, off the top of my head. Just take it easy, son. Didn't mean to insult you."

"Why did you lie to Reynard?" Daniels asked. "I could understand not telling him anything at first, but then that yarn you spun for him . . ."

"That little Frenchy's 'bout the stupidest thing I seen lately," Buffalo said, his voice little more than a whisper. Even at that level, the words were still rather loud and gravelly. "Figgered if I told him some story that was farfetched enough, he'd believe it. Looks like I was right. I was just stallin' at first, seein' what he'd do. Way things were goin', though, I decided he might be dumb enough to shoot us if we didn't tell him *somethin'*."

"Why not the truth?" Rafael asked. "I hate to cooperate with those damned Europeans, but—"

Buffalo shook his head, cutting off Rafael's comment. "If we'd told Reynard the truth, he'd've shot Daniels here for sure, and probably me, too. Maybe even you, too, Rafe."

"Rafael," the Mexican said tightly.

"Whatever. By spinnin' that yarn, we bought a little time, time enough to steal some guns and supplies and horses and get after Guerrero."

"Reynard's planning to go after Guerrero," Daniels pointed out.

"Reynard don't strike me as the kind of feller who can find his own butt," Buffalo snorted. "An' the three of us will be able to move a lot faster than a whole troop of soldiers. Once we get away from here, we won't have to worry about Reynard anymore."

Buffalo seemed to know what he was talking about, so Daniels sighed and nodded. Following the big man's lead was the only course of action that he could see. "Reckon I'm with you," he said.

"And I as well," Rafael added, although he sounded even less enthusiastic than Daniels.

Buffalo grinned in the dim light. "Cheer up, boys. We got us a chance to rescue them gals, pay back Guerrero for what he done, and turn a tidy profit on top of it."

Daniels frowned. "Profit? What kind of profit?"

"With Don Hortensio and Don Antonio both dead, there's a good chance that Doña Isabella is a mighty wealthy woman now. And the don's family would probably pay a good price to whoever was to bring her back safe and sound. Just out of gratitude, you understand."

Rafael's breath was indrawn sharply. "You intend to steal the don's wife from Guerrero and sell her back to the family yourself!" he accused.

"You're makin' it sound like ransom, Rafe," Buffalo said. "It ain't like that at all."

"No. Of course not."

Daniels kept his mouth shut. What Buffalo was proposing did smack of ransom, and yet the big man's words made sense. Don Hortensio's family probably would be grateful to anyone who could bring back Doña Isabella. He supposed he would have to wait and see how things turned out before he made up his mind what to do about them. But there was one decision he had already made.

He was not going to ride on the wrong side of the law anymore. No matter what had happened in the past, he was no longer a bandit.

"Well, what do we do now?" Daniels asked after a moment of strained silence.

"We wait 'til them soldier boys settle down for the night. Then we get us some guns and a few provisions and a pair o' mules for you and me to ride. Don't much like travelin' at night, but I reckon we can put quite a few miles 'tween us and Reynard by mornin'."

"Do you really think we can steal all those things and get out of camp without anyone seeing us?" Rafael wanted to know.

Buffalo grinned at him. "Sonny, I *know* we can."

Time passed slowly inside the tent. Reynard had not provided any bedrolls for them, but that didn't stop Buffalo from wadding his hat into a ball, sticking it under his head, and stretching out on the ground. "Think I'll rest a mite," he told Daniels, resting a hand on the end of the coarsely woven bag that held the possum. "Keep an eye out for scorpions crawlin' in here, why don't you?"

"You mean I'm standing guard?"

"Figgered that makes the most sense. After all, you done slept most of the afternoon."

"You knocked me out!"

"You wasn't awake, was you?" Buffalo snorted and closed his eyes, the brief argument obviously over as far as he was concerned.

Actually, Daniels didn't feel sleepy, and he was willing to watch for scorpions in the faint light that filtered into the tent. The light became even dimmer as the fire died down somewhat outside. He looked at Rafael, saw that the Mexican's eyes were closed, too, even though he was still sitting up.

Daniels had his doubts about Buffalo's plan, but he had to admit that he hadn't come up with anything better so far. The big man had shown some quick thinking in the way he had handled Reynard. However, the Frenchman was inexperienced in the ways of frontier life; anybody could see that. There were probably any number of children between here and Mexico City who could have fooled Reynard, Daniels mused.

He'd never given much thought to the conflict between Maximilian and the *Juaristas*, but if Reynard was a sample of the kind of officer the Emperor had put in charge of the army, it was only a matter of time until Juarez's rebels won this war. It didn't matter to Daniels either way. He couldn't go home, had nothing really to go home to except trouble. As long as he was going to be an outcast anyway, it didn't much matter who was in charge in Mexico City.

He shifted slightly and saw Buffalo Newcomb crack open one eye. Buffalo was a mighty light sleeper, Daniels thought. Probably had to be to have lived so long out here. Within a minute, Buffalo was snoring again. Daniels chuckled. Talk about drawing trouble down on them! That rumble was loud enough to be heard on the other side of the Rio Grande.

Rio Grande . . . That was the first time he had used its gringo name in a long time, even in his thoughts. He had cut himself off so completely from the days in Texas that he called the border river what the Mexicans did— Rio Bravo.

Lost in his thoughts, Daniels had no idea how much time had passed when Buffalo quit snoring, sat up, and pulled back the canvas flap over the tent's entrance. Rafael started, shaken from his half-sleep. Daniels peered past Buffalo through the narrow gap and saw that the campfire had burned down considerably now. There were shadows everywhere in the camp.

"Come on," Buffalo breathed.

He moved with surprising silence for such a massive man, Daniels discovered as he left the tent behind Buffalo. Carrying the possum in its bag, Buffalo stepped to the side and let Daniels and Rafael get ahead of him, not forgetting even now that he intended to keep a close eye on them for any sign of treachery. With a curt gesture, he indicated to his companions that they should head for the back of the row of tents.

Daniels caught a glimpse of a sentry as he ducked behind the tent they had just left. The soldier was on his feet, but his head was resting on his chest and he swayed slightly as he dozed. The other sentries were probably being just as lackadaisical in their duties. At least that was what Buffalo seemed to be counting on.

The mules, both the pack animals and the mounts on

which the soldiers rode, were tied on the other side of
the camp. Buffalo, Daniels, and Rafael crept toward
them. When they reached the last tent in line, Buffalo
held out a hand for them to stop. He pointed to three
rifles stacked in a pyramid shape in front of the tent.
Daniels nodded and jerked a thumb at his chest. Buffalo
considered for a moment, then returned the nod. He
waved Rafael on toward the mules and the piles of packs
on the ground nearby.

Cautiously, Daniels picked up the rifles, being careful
not to let them bang together and raise a racket. In a
crouching run, he hurried to join Buffalo and Rafael.
The big man reached out to take one of the rifles, grimacing as he hefted the lightweight, single-shot musket.
It wasn't much of a weapon, but it was the best they
were going to find here:

"Make sure there's plenty of powder and ball for
these Mississippi rifles," he told Rafael as the Mexican
slung packs on a couple of the mules. Rafael's own pack
animal was nearby; the supplies it had carried had been
thoughtlessly left on its back. That carelessness on the
part of the soldiers was going to come in handy for the
three of them, though.

Buffalo saddled Rafael's horse and two mules. When
he was finished, he signaled for Daniels and Rafael to
mount up.

Daniels was amazed that they had gotten this far without anyone raising an alarm. Discipline had to be non-
existent under Reynard, he thought. It was a good thing
they were taking their leave of this patrol. Sticking with
soldiers like these would be a good way of likely getting
killed in a hurry.

"*Aaieee!*"

The cry made Daniels jerk his head around. One of
the sentries was stumbling toward them, trying to un-
sling his rifle from his back and yelling for them to stop.
"Dammit!" Daniels bit off. He had jinxed them by
thinking about how lucky they had been so far.

"Let's go!" Buffalo rumbled. He dug his heels into

the flanks of his mule and galloped into the darkness. Rafael was right behind him. Each of them led one of the pack animals.

For one harrowing moment, as he grabbed up the reins of the third pack mule and banged his feet against his own mount, Daniels thought that the mule was going to be stubborn and refuse to move. He suppressed a groan of dismay and grated, "Come on, you jug-eared bastard, let's get out of here!"

The mule broke into a backbone-shuddering run.

Daniels pointed it in the same direction Buffalo and Rafael had disappeared. Suddenly, he heard shots behind him. Instinct made him duck forward in the saddle, but if the rifle balls came anywhere near him, they weren't close enough for him to hear. He glanced back as he left the camp behind and saw a few winking flashes of fire.

Wind ruffled his hair as he raced along, keeping a firm grip on the reins of the pack mule. Once he was out of the camp and away from the fire, enough starlight washed down over the plains for him to see where he was going. One of the mules might still step in a hole and break a leg, but a man had to take some chances.

He spotted moving shapes in the darkness up ahead and figured he had found Buffalo and Rafael. Sure enough, the shadowy forms slowed down, and Daniels pulled even with them in a few minutes later. A rumbling voice issued from the larger shape. "You catch any lead, boy?"

Daniels shook his head and said, "Nope. What about you?"

"Me'n Rafe are fine. We'd best get movin' again. I don't think Reynard's goin' to try to come after us in the dark. He won't figger it's worth it for three rifles and a few supplies. He won't like losin' the mules, but I don't reckon he'll miss 'em enough to try to take 'em back."

"He may follow us with the soldiers tomorrow," Rafael said.

"Let him. He won't be able to keep up. 'Sides, I

reckon that patrol won't last another week out here without gettin' ambushed by somebody. Poor devils are follerin' that Frenchman right into hell.''

Buffalo was echoing what Daniels had thought earlier. It took hard, experienced men to survive in this wilderness. He himself had been lucky so far since leaving Texas, and he knew it.

All he wanted to do now was stay alive long enough to find Guerrero and try to help those girls, and maybe to even the score with the bandit leader in the process. He still wasn't sure what all of Buffalo's motives were, but they were likely something to do with money. That was all right. Daniels doubted that either he or Rafael would stand a chance of settling things with Guerrero on their own. And even though he had only known the big, bearded man for a few hours, there was one thing Curtis Daniels was sure of.

He sure as hell wouldn't want Buffalo Newcomb after *him*.

FIVE

BUFFALO STEERED THEM BY the stars, heading north for a ways, then swinging west toward the Sierra Madre when they hit a rockier patch of ground.

"Unless Reynard's got a good tracker with him, which ain't likely, there's at least a chance he'll lose our trail here," Buffalo explained. "Like I said, them soldiers can't keep up with us, but there ain't no point in leavin' 'em an easy trail to foller, neither."

Daniels grimaced as he shifted in the saddle. They weren't galloping the mules anymore, so the pace wasn't quite so teeth rattling, but until a man got used to a mule's gait, it was jarring and hard on a body no matter how fast the animal was going.

Rafael had to be tired, too, even though he was on horseback. He said, "Are we going to ride all night without resting, Señor Buffalo?"

"We'll stop after a spell. Don't want to underestimate that French feller too much. Even a damn fool can get lucky."

Daniels glanced up at the sky. Already, it was starting to pale with false dawn in the east. That would pass, then there would be an hour of deeper darkness than before, and then the real dawn would approach. The wind moving down from the mountains and across the plains was light, but there was a definite chill in it. Daniels would almost be glad to see the warm sun again.

Considering everything that had happened yesterday, he thought, he was very lucky to be alive to be looking forward to dawn.

The air got even colder. Finally, Buffalo reined in and said, "All right, we'd best stop for a while and rest the mules. Don't want to wear these old boys out."

He swung down from the saddle, taking along the bag which he had tied to the horn earlier. As Daniels and Rafael dismounted, Buffalo opened the bag to let Stink wander around for a few minutes.

Rafael watched the possum for a moment as it scuttled along the ground, then said, "Aren't you afraid he will run off?"

Buffalo waved a hand at their surroundings, which were starting to become visible in the growing light. "Where would he go? Possums're damn near blind, and they're slower'n molasses in December. He ain't goin' to get away. Not that he'd want to, mind you. He's too lazy to shift for hisself. Gotten used to bein' fed, just like a dog will."

"How'd you come to have a possum for a pet, anyway?" Daniels asked. "I never heard tell of anybody keeping one before."

"Well, that's a long story, son. Done wrote me a song about it, in fact. I'll sing 'er for you some other time, when I'm in more of a singin' mood."

"I'll look forward to it," Daniels said dryly, imagining what Buffalo's washboard voice would sound like raised in song.

There were canteens on the mules, and Buffalo passed one of them around with orders to drink sparingly. This land wasn't really desert, but water was scarce enough that a man had to be careful how he used it.

"What about some coffee and breakfast?" Daniels asked, but Buffalo shook his head.

"We ain't got time to cook coffee, an' we don't want the smoke from a fire showin', neither. There's tortillas in that pack; you can chaw on some o' them for break-fast.''

A few minutes later, he had them moving again. This time, though, they walked and led the mules. They would mount up again in a few miles, Buffalo said. This way, they could still make some progress but give the mules a little extra rest at the same time. Rafael muttered under his breath about the indignity of being forced to walk—not to mention the aches and pains it caused in a man accustomed to riding—but Daniels kept his mouth shut. For the time being, anyway, he was willing to do what Buffalo Newcomb told him.

The sun crested the horizon behind them and seemed to shoot up into the sky. Within a half hour, Daniels found it hard to believe he had been wishing for the sun's warmth such a short time earlier. The hard, brassy light washed over them, bringing with it a heat that sucked the water from a man's body and made his brain slow down. Daniels found himself lurching along in the saddle in a half-dazed state. Glancing over at Rafael Vasquez, he saw that the Mexican was in the same condition. They were lucky they had the large-brimmed sombreros to provide some shade. Otherwise their brains would have been fried by mid-morning, Daniels thought sluggishly.

Buffalo kept them moving. The heat didn't seem to bother him, even in the poncho he wore. Sweat shone on his face and trickled into his beard, but his eyes were clear and alert. It was a good thing, too, Daniels figured, because he and Rafael weren't worth a damn at the moment.

The terrain through which they were riding was more rugged than it looked at first glance. The landscape appeared to be gently rolling plains that gradually led to the foothills of the mountains, but that was deceiving. You couldn't see the many rocky-bottomed arroyos that cut through the earth until you were right on top of them. Some of the washes had slopes gentle enough for the mules to negotiate without any trouble, but the sides of others were steep enough to force them to detour a mile or more before they found a caved-in spot that would allow them access to the arroyo. Then they might have to ride another mile before finding a place where they could get out on the other side. Buffalo was still heading in a generally westerly direction, but that was the best they could do.

Once, in the middle of the day, while they were riding down one of those arroyos, the big man suddenly held up his hand and signaled for them to stop. Rafael opened his mouth to ask a question, but Buffalo cut him off with a slashing motion. Daniels remained silent, his brain stirring enough to make him a little more alert. Buffalo seemed to be listening intently to something.

Daniels had no idea how long they sat there. It seemed like a long time. But finally Buffalo nodded and said in a low rumble, "All right. Reckon we can go on now."

"What was that about?" Rafael demanded. "I thought we were going to sit here in this hellhole and sweat the rest of our lives away."

"The rest of your life could've been mighty short, sonny, happen we'd kept goin' like we was."

"You heard something, didn't you?" Daniels asked as he got his mule moving again.

"More mules or horses," Buffalo answered. "Sounded like horses. Probably a band of Apaches."

Rafael snorted. "That is ridiculous! I did not hear a thing. Yet you not only hear these phantom horses, Señor Buffalo, but you know too that they belong to Apaches!"

Buffalo didn't say anything for a long moment, then, "Well, could be you're right about the Apache part, Rafe. I don't know that for sure. They might've been *Juaristas*, maybe even another one of the emperor's patrols. But let me ask you this, boy—you got any friends out here in these parts?"

Rafael grimaced and shook his head. "No. No, I suppose I do not have any friends out here. Your point is well taken, señor."

"You sure they moved on?"

Buffalo nodded in response to Daniels's question. "I waited 'til it had been a while since I heard 'em 'fore I said we could move on. Reckon we're safe enough for a spell. We start seein' Apache sign, though, we'll know we got to ride mighty light in the saddle from then on. We might be able to talk *Juaristas* out of killin' us, at least for a while, but not Apaches."

"I am not afraid of a bunch of savages," Rafael said haughtily, but Daniels thought he heard a hint of nervousness under the young Mexican's bravado.

As for himself, he knew good and well he was afraid of the Indians. He'd heard too many stories about Apache torture to be otherwise.

"I'll mind you said that, son," Buffalo replied solemnly to Rafael's comment. "We do happen to run into any of 'em, you can do the parleyin'."

He heeled his mule into motion again, riding down the arroyo and leaving behind a decidedly more uneasy-looking Rafael. Daniels tried not to grin as he followed Buffalo.

Somehow the day passed. Daniels spent much of the time dozing in his saddle, letting Buffalo worry about where they were going and what was happening around them. Maybe that wasn't too smart, trusting your life to a near stranger, the Texan thought, but he was too tired to do anything else. Besides, if Buffalo wanted him dead, there had been plenty of chances before now to accomplish that very thing.

They camped that night in a small bowl in the earth, and once again Buffalo refused to let them have a fire. "Cold camp never hurt nobody," he said. "It ain't near as uncomfortable as losin' your hair."

Daniels would have liked some coffee, but what he really wanted was to stretch out on the ground and ease his aching muscles, to actually sleep the way a man was supposed to sleep. The pounding headache had come back to him, a result of exhaustion and heat and being punched in the face by Buffalo Newcomb the day before. His jaw was still sore, which made chewing the tortillas a little difficult. But he managed; he was hungry enough not to let some pain slow him down.

"Lord, I'm tired," he said as he washed down a tortilla with a swig of canteen water. "I think I could sleep for a week."

Buffalo snorted. He was sitting cross-legged on the ground, with Stink wandering around nearby. A few feet away, Rafael sat with his back against a small boulder, seemingly as exhausted as Daniels was.

"Hell, today weren't nothin', boy," Buffalo said. "Leastways you had a good mule to ride. When we was bein' marched from Mier to Mexico City, back in '43, we was on foot and draggin' the chains they had on us, too."

Rafael lifted his head in interest. "You were at Mier when they drew the beans?"

"Yep. Seems now like a damn fool stunt, ridin' down here like some sort of real army, but we figgered we'd be able to pick up plenty of booty along the way and then rescue them Texas boys the Mexes had in their dungeon." Buffalo glanced at Rafael. "No offense, son. You can't help it that Santa Anna was such a blood-thirsty bastard. Reckon he never got over the lickin' he took at the Alamo and San Jacinto."

"The battle at San Antonio de Bexar was a great victory for Santa Anna and his army," Rafael said stiffly. Night had fallen, so Daniels couldn't see the young Mexican's face. It was clear, though, that he was insulted by Buffalo's comments.

"Victory? Not the way us Texians saw it. San Jacinto might've been the last nail in the old boy's coffin, but the Alamo was the first one." Buffalo waved a hand. "Hell, Rafe, don't get all het up about it. It was a long time ago, an' I done said it was foolish for Somervell to lead that expedition down here in '42. By that time, though, I reckon we was just in the habit of gettin' into scrapes with the Mexicans. Figgered one more wouldn't hurt."

Daniels had heard the story of the black beans and how one in ten of the captives had been executed by a firing squad. The survivors had been taken to Mexico City and imprisoned. "How did you get out of that dungeon?" he asked Buffalo. "The way I heard it, a lot of the prisoners died there."

"They sure did. Them that were left got to figgerin' that we'd all die sooner or later if we didn't get out of there. So a few of us got together and dug us a tunnel out of there."

"Ridiculous!" Rafael said. "I have never heard of anyone escaping from that prison."

Buffalo shrugged, the motion visible even in the starlight. "Reckon Santa Anna must've hushed it up 'cause he didn't want nobody to know we'd got away. But I'm here to tell you, son, it happened. We dug out of that dungeon and lit out north for Texas. Took a while to get there, but some of us made it."

"With all the trouble you've had down here, why did you ever come back?" Daniels asked. He was getting very sleepy now, but his curiosity was enough to keep him awake for a few moments longer.

"Shoot, I love the place. Ain't no finer people on earth than the regular folks in Mexico. It's the damned politicians and the dictators who take turns messin' the place up." Daniels could not see Buffalo's grin, but he could hear it in the big man's voice as he went on, "There's some of the purtiest women and best liquor in the world down here. Man'd be a fool to stay away just 'cause a few folks tried to kill him a time or two."

What Buffalo said made sense, and it ended the discussion as far as Daniels was concerned. Rafael was not willing to let it go, however. He said, "My father was an officer in Santa Anna's army. He was at the Alamo and San Jacinto."

"That don't make no nevermind to me. Santa Anna was the one runnin' the show. Your pa just did what his boss told him to do. I don't bear no grudges against a man like that . . . or his boy."

Rafael drew a deep breath. "But—"

"Howsomever, I do get a mite riled when I'm tryin' to sleep an' somebody keeps yappin' at me." Buffalo stretched out, his head on his saddle roll, and tipped the black hat down over his face. "You got the first watch, Rafe. I'll take the second, and Daniels can have the last. Keep your eyes open. Like I said, we ain't got no friends out here."

That was the last thing Daniels heard as he drifted off to sleep.

It seemed like only ten minutes had passed when something touched Daniels on the shoulder. His eyes snapped open and saw something huge and dark blotting out the stars in the sky above him. He started to sit up abruptly, but a big hand on his shoulder stopped him. After a few seconds, he realized the bulky shape was Buffalo Newcomb.

"Take it easy, boy," Buffalo said. "It'll be dawn in a little while. Figgered I'd get a little more sleep 'fore it's time to ride."

He let Daniels sit up this time. The Texan drew a deep breath, stretched, knuckled his eyes as he tried to wake up fully. Another glance at the stars and the eastern sky told him that dawn was a couple of hours off. Buffalo had let him sleep past the usual time for the shift of the third man on watch to begin.

"Thanks," he grunted, figuring that Buffalo would know what he was doing.

"*De nada*. I'm used to not gettin' as much sleep as some folks." Buffalo settled down again and started to snore almost immediately.

Daniels reached over and picked up his rifle, cradling it in his arms as he got a drink from the canteen by his side. His eyeballs felt gritty and the hard ground had aggravated his aches and pains, rather than easing them, but he was wide awake.

He didn't rouse Buffalo and Rafael until the sun was bursting over the horizon. Buffalo groused a little about burning daylight while they ate another cold meal and saddled their mounts, but they were on the move again less than a half hour after dawn, rocking along in their saddles, the possum riding in the bag again. Buffalo had cut two holes in it so that the little animal's snout and tail could stick out as he rode.

Daniels looked up at the Sierra Madre as he rode. The mountains didn't seem any closer than they had been the day before, and neither did the foothills. It would take them several more days to reach the hills, he decided. Even at this distance, though, the view was spectacular— the gray heights thrusting up from the flatlands, white clouds looming over them against the deep blue sky. He would be glad when they reached the mountains.

Around midmorning, Buffalo called a halt and pointed out some tracks that crossed their path at an angle. "No shoes on those ponies," he said. "Them's Apaches, all right."

Rafael had been unusually quiet this morning. Now he said, "Señor Buffalo, I . . . I did not tell you something when I woke you to stand guard last night. While you and Daniels were asleep, I thought I heard something."

Buffalo turned sharply in his saddle to face the Mexican. "You did what?" he demanded.

"I thought I heard something. I started to wake you, but then the noise stopped."

Buffalo was glaring. "What kind of noise?"

"I . . . I do not really know. The whisper of feet on sand, perhaps."

Buffalo spat out a heartfelt curse. "That was Injuns, boy. They slipped up to see who we was. Reckon we must've got 'em curious about us, else they'd've killed us last night." He looked around at the near wasteland surrounding them. "They're prob'ly hangin' back a mile or two, stayin' out of sight while they trail us. Dammit!"

"What do you think they'll do?" Daniels asked.

"No tellin'. Nine times out o' ten, they'd've just killed us outright. Now they prob'ly want to see what we're up to. Once a Injun gets curious, he's liable to poke around at somethin' for a long time 'fore he does anything.''

"Perhaps we can elude them," Rafael suggested.

"Not very damn likely," Buffalo replied flatly. He scowled at Rafael. "Boy, next time you hear *anything*, even if it turns out to be just a Gila monster breakin' wind, you damn well better tell me!''

"I will, Señor Buffalo," Rafael promised.

Buffalo gestured with his rifle. "Come on. We might as well keep movin' whilst we got the chance.''

No one bothered them as they rode, and by noon Daniels was beginning to wonder if Buffalo had overestimated the threat. That didn't seem likely, considering the man's experience, but anybody could make a mistake, even Buffalo Newcomb. Maybe there weren't any Apaches within fifty miles.

Lunch was jerky and tortillas again, eaten while they paused briefly to rest the mules and Rafael's horse. Daniels was getting tired of that diet, but there wasn't much they could do about it as long as there were Indians in the vicinity. The tortillas they had stolen from the Mexican camp would be running out soon, however. Once that happened, they might have to risk a fire.

Buffalo scanned their back trail, looking for any sign of pursuit by Captain Reynard and his troops. After a few minutes, the big man grunted and said, "No dust anywhere that I can see. Like I said, ol' Reynard prob'ly figgered it weren't worth it to come after us. Reckon he's gone back to Mexico City to try to explain to Maximilian how Don Hortensio and his boy got theirselves killed whilst Reynard was off chasin' phantom *Juaristas*.''

"You think there were no *Juaristas* in the area?" Rafael asked.

"Don't matter if there was or not. Folks sometimes see rebels where there ain't none, just to confuse the emperor's boys. Even if they was there, a feller like Reynard ain't likely to be able to catch 'em.''

"True." Rafael sighed. "Emperor Maximilian has made some bad choices when it comes to the men in command of his army. For every skillful general like Woll, there are a dozen incompetent Captain Reynards."

Buffalo grinned. "I'm a mite surprised to hear you talkin' like that, Rafe. I had you figgered for a member of the landed gentry. And they like Maximilian, since he's let 'em keep most of their holdin's."

"My family is conservative politically," Rafael admitted. "My older brothers have always backed Maximilian, ever since Napoléon III sent him here. If my father was still alive, I do not know what he would do, but he has been dead for ten years. He did not live to see the evil times that have fallen on our land."

Rafael sounded like he didn't agree with the rest of his relatives when it came to Maximilian, Daniels thought. That was surprising, considering that he came from a well-to-do family. But the Mexican was certainly no *Juarista*, either. Maybe he didn't know exactly *what* he was.

Daniels wasn't going to spend a lot of time worrying about the question. As far as he was concerned, Rafael was an ally, even if not a very pleasant one. That was just a temporary circumstance, however. Once their business with Guerrero was settled, the three of them would probably go their separate ways. That was fine with Daniels.

They pushed on soon after the meal was finished. Buffalo was watching now for tracks that might have been left by the *bandidos*, but so far there had been no sign of Guerrero and his band.

"Do you think the Apaches would attack Guerrero and his men, Señor Buffalo?" Rafael asked.

"Half a dozen well-heeled hombres?" Buffalo mused. "Well, maybe. If they still got those two gals with 'em, that'd be a powerful lure. Now, if we were talkin' about Comanch', ain't no doubt in my mind they'd try to jump Guerrero's bunch. But I don't know about Apaches. They might have too much sense to risk it, less'n they outnumbered them bandits by quite a bit.''

During the afternoon, they cut more tracks of unshod horses, and Buffalo's frown deepened. During a brief pause, he said, "Maybe we ain't dealin' with Apaches after all. Or maybe not just Apaches. Could be there's more'n one war party out. Don't know what we're ridin' into, boys, but it's shapin' up to be pretty bad.''

Rafael was pale underneath his tan as he said, "Should we turn back?''

"I thought you was anxious to rescue that cousin of your'n.''

"I am, but it is possible that Angelina is not even alive anymore. She would not want me to lose my life as well. . . .''

Daniels said flatly, "I'm not turning back. As long as there's a chance of catching up to Guerrero, I say we go ahead.''

"Turnin' back wouldn't help nobody anyway," Buffalo said, then spat into the dust. "Likely there's Injuns behind us, too, as well as ahead. Only chance we got now of keepin' our hair is to stay together and keep goin'. Could be we'll reach the Sierra Madre before any of those bucks decide to make a move against us. If we do, at least there'll be places up there where we can fort up.''

Daniels nodded, and after a moment Rafael did, too. Harsh though the big man's logic was, he was right. They had to keep moving and hoping. That was all that was left for them.

The optimism Daniels had felt earlier in the day had fled. He was convinced now that they were on the verge of sudden, violent death. There had been other times, while he was riding with Guerrero, that he had been convinced he was about to die. Usually, that had not bothered him very much. Now, though, he was surprised to find that he wanted to live, wanted it a great deal.

Maybe that punch of Buffalo's had knocked some sense into his head, he thought. Either that, or it had totally unhinged him.

Late in the afternoon, Buffalo reined in abruptly and snapped, "You hear that?"

Daniels and Rafael both listened intently. At first Daniels didn't hear anything, but then some faint sounds came drifting to his ears. He frowned and said, "What is it?"

"Somebody's screamin'," Buffalo said grimly. "Come on."

He kicked his mule into a gallop, veering a little south of the course they had been following. Daniels and Rafael followed close behind, dragging the pack mules with them. As he rode, Daniels shifted his grip on the rifle lying across the pommel of his saddle. The musket was already loaded and primed, and he wanted his thumb where it could ear back the hammer in a hurry if necessary.

Buffalo's mule thundered up a small rise. Daniels could still hear the screaming, even over the sound of hoofbeats from their mounts. He wondered what they would find on the other side of that rise. Indians or bandits? And would it really matter?

As they topped the rise, Daniels saw a small adobe jacal on the other side. Nearby was a crude garden patch and the remains of a rickety fence that might have held sheep or goats before something—or someone—had smashed it to kindling. Some poor fool had started a little farm out here in the middle of nowhere.

And he had paid for that audacity with his life. A man lay sprawled in front of the entrance to the hut. There were large bloody wounds on his torso where arrows had pierced his body and then been born back out of his flesh. His head was a gory mess, his scalp gone. The blood that had splashed down and coated his contorted features appeared to be fairly fresh.

Daniels jerked his head around, looking for the Indians who had committed this atrocity. There wasn't a living soul in sight, except for him and his two companions. The savages had done their work and left, taking the farmer's flock with them.

The screams were coming from inside the jacal.

Daniels's skin crawled as he listened to the agonized sounds. At least the farmer was dead, out of his misery. The screams sounded like they were coming from a woman, and Daniels wasn't sure he wanted to know what had been done to her to make her shriek like that. He became aware that he was tightly gripping the rifle, and that his hands were sweating.

Buffalo had reined in near the dead man. His bearded face was expressionless as he said, "You two keep an eye out. I'll go in and see what I can do for the lady."

Daniels knew what Buffalo could do. Chances were, a musket ball through the head would be the most merciful thing.

Buffalo swung down from the saddle and strode into the hut. Daniels and Rafael waited, exchanging a nervous glance as a fresh chorus of shrill screams broke out. Daniels took a deep breath and forced his eyes to scan the horizon. He wanted to concentrate on that task, rather than thinking about what was going to happen inside the crude little house.

Suddenly, when he had been inside less than a minute, Buffalo burst out of the hut, almost running. Daniels's eyes widened, Buffalo looked scared, and Daniels wondered wildly just what the hell could frighten a man like Buffalo Newcomb.

"Get in there, goddamn it!" Buffalo howled at them, his cry blending in with another shriek from inside the hut.

Daniels dropped off his horse, still tightly clutching the rifle. "What is it?" he demanded. "What did they do to the woman?"

Buffalo hurried past him, as walleyed as a spooked horse, and said, "The Injuns didn't do nothin'. She's havin' a *baby*!"

SIX

DANIELS CAUGHT BUFFALO'S ARM and stared at him in amazement for a moment. Finally, he echoed, "A baby?"

"You heard me, dammit! Get in there and help her!"

Daniels glanced at Rafael. "You know anything about babies?"

The Mexican was shaking his head frantically. "No, señor. I know nothing." He was almost as pale as Buffalo.

Daniels took a deep breath. Both of his companions were going to be useless in this situation, he could see. That left it up to him. In fact, he *did* know something about childbirth. He had helped the midwife when his wife had given birth to their two children. Husbands were usually shooed out of the room when the time came, but old Granny Proctor had needed some assistance, and he had been the only one around to help.

"All right," he said, thrusting his rifle into Buffalo's hands. "Hang on to this. I'll see what I can do."

He took a deep breath and strode into the hut. There was only one room, with the door at the front and a tiny window at the back. There was enough light for him to see the pathetic furnishings and the dirt floor. A table and a chair were to his right, and to his left was a narrow bed made of woven rope with a blanket laid over it. The woman on the bed was lying with her legs toward him. Between her widespread knees he could see her head thrown back in agony, her face covered with sweat, the features twisted.

Buffalo had been right. She was definitely having a baby.

Daniels felt a wave of nausea go through him. The interior of the little shack was overpoweringly hot. The woman screamed until she had no more breath, then panted for a few seconds while she gathered her energy.

Calling her a woman was being generous, Daniels saw as he took a hesitant step closer. She probably wasn't any older than fifteen. Her thin arms and legs splayed out on the bunk made her swollen belly look even more enormous than it really was.

Daniels moved beside the bed and knelt so that he could reach out and touch one of her hands as she clutched at the blanket underneath her. She jerked sharply and her eyes, which had been closed, flew open and shone with terror. The scream that tore out of her throat made him flinch.

"Hold it! Hold it!" he told her in Spanish, grabbing her wrist and raising his voice so that she could hear him over her own cries. "I'm a friend! I've come to help you."

"Apache!"

Her voice was choked with fear and pain, but Daniels had no trouble understanding what she said. A shiver touched him. So Buffalo's growing concern had been well-founded. There were Apaches in the area, and from the looks of things, they were the ones who had raided this little farm.

"There are no Indians here now," he said, hoping that his words got through to her. "I'll help you. No Apache. You understand? No Apache."

Slowly, her dark eyes seemed to focus on him. She stopped shrieking—at least for the moment. When the next contractions hit her, she would cry out again, Daniels knew, even if she had figured out by then that he meant her no harm.

Daniels kept hold of her hand and looked quickly around the single room. There was nothing here to help him, none of the things he would need. Turning his head, he shouted, "Buffalo!"

There was no response at first, and Daniels was beginning to wonder if Buffalo was too rattled to even come to the doorway. But then the big man's form loomed against the late afternoon light, and he said nervously, "What?"

"You're going to have to build a fire and heat some water," Daniels said. "And I'll need some clean, dry cloth and a knife. Pass the blade through the fire a few times before you give it to me."

"Where'm I s'posed to find such?" Buffalo demanded.

"I don't know. Just do it!"

Daniels turned his attention back to the woman, not waiting to see if Buffalo did as he was told or not. The young Texan took another deep breath and leaned back to see if the baby was visible yet. He couldn't see the top of its head, and he hoped that was a good sign.

A new spasm shook the woman, and her hand twisted, the fingers grasping Daniels's hand and squeezing with incredible force. He grunted and hung on as the screams rang out again.

He wasn't sure how much time had passed when Buffalo came back into the jacal. Buffalo had an earthen pot filled with hot water in one hand, and there were several pieces of what looked like a horse blanket in his other hand. He set the pot down by the bed and grunted, "Here you go. I'll have that knife for you in a minute. It ain't much. Rafe found it outside, around back. The blade's mighty dull."

"That's all right," Daniels replied. "I just need it to cut the cord. But it has to be clean. That's what the midwife told me when my youngsters were born."

"All right. I'll hold 'er in the fire like you said."

Buffalo hurried back out after dropping the cloths on the foot of the bed. Daniels grabbed one of them up as a fresh contraction made the Mexican woman arch her back away from the bunk. He slipped the cloth underneath her, between her hips and the filthy blanket.

The contractions were almost constant now. That meant the baby would be coming very soon. He moved around to the foot of the bunk and crouched there awkwardly, picking up another piece of cloth and waiting. Out of curiosity, he lifted the material to his nose and sniffed. Definitely a horse blanket, he decided. But it seemed to be fairly clean. It would have to do.

Surrounded by the heat and the cries from the woman, time seemed to stand still for Daniels. He felt as if he had been kneeling inside the hut for hours.

But when the moment came, he was suddenly very busy, trying to do several things at once and wishing that he had another pair of hands. And Buffalo still hadn't come back with the knife, damn him. . . .

"Here it is, Daniels, just like you—"

Daniels heard the heavy footsteps and the rumbling voice behind him, but he couldn't look up, not at the moment. He welcomed the new life into his hands, wrapping it in the cloth, using another piece to clean the tiny mouth and nose. Then, moving quickly, the way he remembered Granny Proctor doing it, he upended the baby and gave its wrinkled rear end a sharp smack.

The gasping for breath as new reflexes struggled to work abruptly became an indignant howl. Daniels felt his face stretching into a huge grin as he cradled the baby again and leaned forward to place it in its mother's arms. The young woman was still panting from the effort she had put forth, but she took the child eagerly.

"Sheee-it!" Buffalo Newcomb said.

Daniels stood up, still grinning. He saw the astounded look on Buffalo's face and said, "Don't tell me you've never seen a baby being born before?"

The big man shook his shaggy head. "No, sir, I ain't. I've seen cows and horses and pigs havin' young'uns, but this here is a whole 'nother thing, ain't it?"

"I suppose so." Daniels held out his hand. "I'll take that knife now."

Buffalo nodded distractedly and gave him the little blade. Daniels cut the cord and then set about cleaning up the mess that went with childbirth. Slowly, Buffalo backed out of the hut, still flabbergasted by what he had seen.

In the two days that he had known Buffalo, Daniels thought, the man had proven himself to be a tireless rider, a good tracker, and a highly efficient killer of men. It was good to know that there were still a few things that could throw even a ring-tailed wonder like Buffalo Newcomb for a loop.

When he was done, he wiped his hands on the last piece of cloth and then stood beside the bunk, looking down at the woman and the baby. The infant had gone to sleep, nuzzled against its mother's body. Daniels suddenly realized that he hadn't even checked to see whether it was a boy or a girl. He had been too concerned with making sure it was breathing.

The young woman's eyes were closed as well. Daniels bent over, carefully lifting the material that was serving as swaddling clothes. He didn't want to disturb the exhausted mother, but his curiosity was getting the best of him.

The baby was a girl. Daniels smiled. That was good to know. Maybe she would grow up to be a fine woman and have many sons and daughters of her own.

He felt his lips moving and realized that he was offering up a prayer for the first time in . . . well, God knew how long it had been. Daniels certainly didn't. But a long time, anyway. He was praying that the mother and daughter would be strong enough to endure what the future would hold for them. It would be a hard road, he knew.

Looking at the two of them sleeping there so peacefully took him back in his mind to his own home, to the way Willa had looked after Callie was born. It had been much the same after Matt's birth. Something had been different, though, some tiny something that had wound up making all the difference in the world. Pain shot through him as the good memories turned bad. . . .

"*Gracias.*"

The word was whispered so softly that for a second Daniels wasn't sure whether he had really heard it or imagined it. But then he looked down at the young Mexican woman and saw that her eyes were open. She looked from him to the baby and then back to him, her moist eyes meeting his, and she said again, "*Gracias.* Thank you for . . . my baby, señor."

Daniels went down to one knee beside the bunk and reached out to gently stroke the baby's cheek. He smiled and told the woman, "You did the work, señora. I just sort of tidied up after you."

Her head moved back and forth slightly. "No. I owe everything to you." Her still-sweaty forehead creased in a frown. "I thought there were Indians. . . . I remember awful noises. . . ."

Daniels shook his head emphatically. "No Indians," he said. "There's no Indians anywhere around here." That might be a lie, but it was what she needed to hear right now. Maybe she would let it go at that.

"Alejandro," she said after a moment. "Has Alejandro seen the baby yet?"

Daniels hesitated. He had been hoping she would sleep awhile before he had to tell her that her man was dead.

"Alejandro, that's your husband?" he asked.

"*Sí.* Alejandro Salazar. I am Margarita Salazar. And this"—she looked down at the sleeping infant—"this is Antonia."

"Pleased to meet you," he smiled. "I'm Curtis Daniels."

"You are . . . a gringo?"

He realized that the sun had gone down, that dusk was throwing thick shadows into the hut. She hadn't known until he introduced himself that he wasn't a Mexican.

"That's right. I'm from Texas."

"You are . . . a long way from home, señor."

That was the truth, Daniels thought. And the truth usually hurt. But you couldn't get away from it, not in this life. "Señora Salazar, I have to tell you something," he began. "There were Indians here earlier. Apaches, from the looks of things."

"*Aaieee*," she breathed, her eyes widening in the gloom. "Then the things I heard, they were real?"

Daniels nodded.

"The baby began to come, and then Alejandro heard something outside," she went on. "He went out to see what it was. . . . There was a shot. . . . Alejandro had an old rifle, you see . . . and then terrible noises . . ." Margarita Salazar lifted herself on an elbow, staring into Daniels's face. "My husband . . . Oh, *Dios*, no!"

"I'm sorry," Daniels said, knowing how useless it was to say it. "Your husband is dead."

Margarita sank back down on the bunk, her eyes closed, her lips working in a prayer. Then a sob shook her, and another, and for several minutes she cried.

Then she lifted the arm that was not cuddling the baby and used the back of her hand to wipe away the tears from her face. "I have cried for my husband and my daughter and . . . and myself," she said. "I will pray much for all of us. I wish at this moment that I was dead along with Alejandro. But I must live, Señor Daniels. I must live for my daughter, for Antonia."

"What you need to do right now is get some sleep," Daniels told her. "My friends and I will watch the place and . . . and take care of everything. You and Antonia rest."

"*Sí.*"

Daniels started to turn away, but she stopped him by saying softly, "Señor Daniels . . . thank you again."

He nodded and went out, not knowing what else to say to her.

Buffalo and Rafael were waiting for him, anxious expressions on their faces in the light from the small fire Buffalo had made. "Well?" the big man demanded. "Are they goin' to be all right?"

"As far as I can tell," Daniels replied. "The baby seems healthy enough, and the woman is stronger than she looks."

"But what are we going to do with them?" Rafael asked. He swept a hand to indicate the devastated farm. "They cannot stay here alone."

"No, they can't," Daniels agreed. "But we've got something else to take care of first, before we worry about that."

Buffalo nodded. "Yep. And you're elected, Rafe."

"Me?" Rafael exclaimed. "I am no gravedigger."

"You are now, son," Buffalo said flatly. "Daniels just delivered hisself a baby, so I reckon he's tired, and I dug the last batch. There's a little shovel on one of them pack mules. Was I you, I'd get busy. This ground's mighty hard, and it's liable to take a while."

Buffalo was right. It took a long time for Rafael to dig a grave for Alejandro Salazar. Finally, Daniels began to feel sorry for the Mexican as he watched Rafael scraping at the stony earth, so he volunteered to take over. Rafael gladly handed the shovel to him, and Daniels took it despite a disapproving look from Buffalo.

When it was done, Daniels went back into the hut to check on Margarita and little Antonia. Both of them were sleeping soundly. As he emerged from the jacal, he nodded to Buffalo and said quietly, "We might as well get it done."

He had been carefully avoiding looking at the body. It was too gruesome a sight even for his hardened sensibilities. Buffalo got to his feet, went over to Salazar's corpse, and hefted it casually, not seeming to worry about getting any more blood on him. The big man had regained his composure. Witnessing a baby being born might make him wide-eyed and jelly-kneed, but carrying the body of a scalped, arrow-riddled dead man didn't bother him a bit.

The grave was not overly deep, maybe four feet, and was only long enough for Salazar to fit into it. The ground was just too hard and rocky to make it any bigger. Daniels hoped it would be good enough.

"You goin' to get the widow out here and say words over him, Daniels?" Buffalo asked.

A humorless smile plucked at Daniels's mouth. He had already functioned as a doctor today; now Buffalo wanted him to be a preacher, too. "She needs the rest," he said. "Let's just let her sleep. But I'll say the words anyway."

Buffalo had torn strips off a spare horse blanket that had been in one of Rafael's packs to furnish the cloths for Daniels. About half of the blanket was left, and they wrapped Salazar's body in it as best they could. Then Buffalo lowered it into the grave, and Daniels and Rafael began scraping the earth back into the hole, Daniels with the shovel, Rafael with his bare hands. Covering the grave didn't take nearly as long as digging it.

When they were done and there was a small mound of dirt to mark Alejandro Salazar's resting place, Daniels stood over the grave, his chest heaving from exertion, and said, "Lord, we're sending this man on to you. We don't know much about him—he was a farmer, and his name was Alejandro Salazar. He had a wife named Margarita, and now a baby named Antonia. You know all this a lot better than we do. But I reckon he was probably a good man, and we hope you'll take care of him and his family, too. Amen."

"Amen," Rafael repeated softly.

Buffalo had taken his old black hat off while Daniels was speaking. Now he clapped it back on his head and said, "We'd best get that fire out. We've already told ever'body for twenty miles around that we're here by burnin' it as long as we have."

"If we have already revealed our presence, Señor Buffalo, why should we not keep the fire burning and enjoy its warmth?" Rafael asked as he turned away from the grave and followed Buffalo. "We could have coffee and warm food."

"If we put out the fire, maybe some of the folks who been watchin' us will figger we done left," Buffalo replied. "That way, if we stay here tonight, they'll look for us some other place." He shook his head. "It ain't much to hope for, but it's better'n nothing."

He scooped sand on the fire and put it out, and as Daniels watched the embers die, he wished, like Rafael, that they had heated some water earlier for coffee. But they had all been busy, himself most of all.

It had been quite a day, he thought as he settled down with his back against the wall of the hut next to the doorway. His eyelids drooped as tiredness caught up with him.

It wasn't every day that a man helped to bring a new life into the world, he thought with a smile. The feeling was a good one. It beat taking lives out of the world all to pieces.

S✷E✷V✷E✷N

THE SCREAM WOKE DANIELS up. He bolted to his feet, grabbing the rifle beside him. Shaking his head in an attempt to clear it, he searched the darkness that surrounded him. There was no sign of trouble.

Once again, the cry ripped through the night, and this time he could tell it came from inside the hut. Wheeling around, he plunged through the opening. He thought wildly that the Apaches might have come back and snuck into the jacal through the tiny window in the back wall.

The shadows were so thick inside the hut he couldn't make out a thing except the rectangle of faint light that marked the position of the window. Daniels knew if he spoke, he would be giving away his own location, but he hissed, "Margarita!"

A whimper came from his left, from where the bunk was. Daniels moved in that direction, holding the rifle in his right hand and feeling in front of him with the left. He crouched, sweeping the hand in front of him, and touched the woman on the shoulder. Instantly, she clutched at him.

"Señor Daniels!" she gasped. "Is it you?"

"That's right, Margarita," he said, trying to keep his voice calm. His nerves were jumping around like bugs on a hot rock. "What happened? What's wrong?"

The baby wailed. Daniels heard the rustle of fabric shifting around, and then Margarita sat up. "It is all right," she said a little breathlessly. "I . . . I was dreaming."

A big shape cut off what little starlight filtered through the door. "You in here, Daniels?" Buffalo asked.

"Yeah," he answered, listening to his pulse pound in his head. It was slowing down gradually as the near panic wore off. "Everything's fine, Buffalo. Señora Salazar just had a bad dream."

Buffalo grunted and moved away from the door. Daniels wished he had a light of some sort. The baby was still fretting, but she fell silent abruptly, the cries being replaced by soft sucking sounds.

"Ah, she was hungry," Margarita said, her own voice more normal now. "I hope I did not frighten you, Señor Daniels."

"Don't worry about that," he told her, feeling suddenly embarrassed to know that the young woman was nursing her baby only a few inches away from him. He started to stand up, but her fingers caught at his sleeve again.

"Please stay," she asked quietly. "The darkness . . . it is evil when you are alone."

"Antonia is here," he pointed out.

"That is not the same, señor. I hate to ask it of you, since you have done so much for us already, but if you would just stay until the *niño* is asleep again . . ."

Daniels took a deep breath. "Sure," he said. "I'll stay."

He sat there holding Margarita's hand while the baby nursed, hoping that the uncomfortable feeling would go away. It didn't. He had always enjoyed being around while Willa nursed their children, but that had been entirely different.

Finally, the baby was finished and quickly fell asleep again. Margarita squeezed Daniels's hand and whispered, *"Gracias."* He slid his fingers out of hers and stood up.

"Try to get some more sleep," he said, then went to the door and out of the hut without looking back.

Blowing out his breath, he stood there for a moment. The rifle dangled beside him from his right hand. He could see a dark shape next to the wall that he took to be Rafael sleeping. The cries had not disturbed the bone-tired Mexican.

"Ever'thing all right?"

The question made Daniels jump slightly. He hadn't heard Buffalo come up beside him. There was something wrong about a man of his size being able to move so quietly.

"Sure," he said. "The lady just had a nightmare. Reckon I might, too, if I had been through everything she has." Daniels glanced up at the sky and figured it was at least four o'clock in the morning. He said, "You let me sleep late again."

Buffalo shrugged. "Like I said, it don't matter that much to me." He paused, then went on, "You was in there for a while."

"She wanted me to stay while she fed the baby. She was scared of the dark." Daniels's voice took on a sharper edge. "That was all it amounted to, Newcomb."

"Hell, don't be so touchy, boy. Didn't mean nothin'. Have to admit you got me curious, though. Didn't hardly pay no attention to it yesterday afternoon, what with ever'thing else goin' on, but I recollect now you sayin' somethin' about havin' a wife and kids your ownself. That true?"

Daniels felt his face go tight as Buffalo asked the question, and his chest suddenly felt as if there was a band around it. "Most folks know better than to ask a man too many questions about where he's been and what he's done."

"Oh, I know better, but I got this here pesky curiosity. An' I figger it's a good thing to know as much as you can 'bout a feller you're ridin' with."

"I thought I was just one step above a prisoner,"
Daniels pointed out. "You kept telling me how you were
going to watch me like a hawk in case I tried to double-
cross you somehow."

Buffalo spat. "I've rode with you for two days now.
You can learn a lot about a feller in two days. I ain't
sayin' I trust you whole hog, but I reckon you ain't
really the treacherous sort. For one thing, you know me
well enough by now to figger that I'll kill you, happen
you try anything."

Daniels had a chuckle at the big man's reasoning. "I
suppose you're right," he said. "That still doesn't mean
I want to talk about my past."

"Fair enough. Didn't figger it'd hurt to ask." Buffalo
canted his rifle over his shoulder. "Since you're awake,
I might as well get some shut-eye myself."

"That's fine," Daniels told him. "I don't think I
could go back to sleep now, anyway."

Buffalo faded off into the shadows and Daniels sat
down with his back against the wall again. The cold
night air and the knowledge that Indians might be watching the place at that very moment made a shiver go
through him. He set the rifle down beside him and pulled
his knees up.

There hadn't been a sound from inside the hut since
he had left it. He hoped Margarita had dozed off again.
He frowned as he wondered what they were going to do
with her and the baby. They couldn't just ride off and
leave them here, alone and defenseless, but would Margarita and Antonia be any safer traveling with the three
of them? After all, they were on the trail of a ruthless
bandit and possibly being followed by Indians themselves. Daniels had no idea where the nearest village
was, but if they could find some sort of settlement, even
if it was just a mission, that would probably be the best
solution. They could leave Margarita and Antonia there,
with people who would care for them and protect them.

Unless they were lucky enough to find such a place,
though, the young woman and her baby would have to

accompany them wherever the trail might lead.

Things could change in an all-fired hurry, Daniels thought as he waited for dawn to arrive. His own life was a prime example of that. You thought things were going along just fine, and then they blew up right in your face. That was what had happened to him, and he had been left to pick up the pieces of a shattered life.

So far, he hadn't done a very good job of it, he told himself.

He wished the sun would come up. He thought too much in the dark like this.

Daniels did the worst thing he could have possibly done: he went to sleep.

The last thing he remembered was the sky beginning to turn gray in the east. Then he realized that his head was down and his eyes were closed.

Jerking erect, he opened his eyes and saw movement in front of him. There was a flash of reddish-brown skin, a flicker of bright color, the sudden glint of sunlight on metal.

An Apache brave was lunging at him, knife upraised and about to drive into his chest.

Daniels let out a yell and dove to the side. The knife hit the adobe only inches above him. His hand slapped the stock of the rifle as he rolled frantically, hitting the Indian's legs and knocking them out from under the man.

Daniels plucked the rifle from the ground as he shouted, "Apaches!"

The one who had tried to knife him scrambled back onto his feet and twisted to throw himself after Daniels. The Texan tipped the barrel of the rifle up as his finger found the trigger guard of the weapon. There was no time to aim, no time to do anything except pull the trigger.

The musket blasted, sending its ball tearing through the belly of the Apache. He spun crazily, then fell, dying without a sound.

Daniels barely had time to think that the Indian must

have made some slight sound while rushing him and that the noise had been what woke him, when the soft slap of more footsteps came from behind him. He came up on one knee and twisted at the waist, lashing out with the now-empty rifle. The barrel caught another onrushing Apache across the midsection, doubling him over. Daniels lunged at the savage and drove his shoulder into the man's thighs.

Both men fell to the ground, but Daniels landed on top. He lifted the rifle and brought it down, smashing the butt into the hate-contorted features beneath him. Two vicious blows made the Apache go limp.

Daniels looked around wildly. Where were Buffalo and Rafael? He heard whoops as more Indians sprang from the brush and ran toward the hut. Inside the jacal, Margarita was screaming again, no doubt roused from sleep by the commotion outside. The sun was up, but just barely. Daniels couldn't have slept very long.

Long enough, he thought grimly. He saw four more Apaches coming toward him, and here he was waiting with an empty gun.

A rifle cracked from the corner of the hut, and one of the Indians went backward as if he had run into a wall. Daniels came to his feet and met the charge of another one, driving him back with a sweeping blow of the rifle. He put too much into it, though, and went too far, leaving him open for an attack before he could recover his balance. A knife blade flickered and burned across his ribs as he tried to jerk away from it.

Daniels dropped the rifle and caught the arm of the Indian who had thrust the knife at him. He fell over backward, but as he did so, he brought his knee up and slammed the Apache's arm across it. There was a sharp crack as bone broke, and the knife went skittering away in the dust.

The Apache got his other hand on Daniels's throat, the fingers closing tightly, brutally. The man was smaller than Daniels, but he had surprising strength. He got his knees on Daniels's belly and crouched there, broken arm dangling uselessly at his side, choking the life out of Daniels one-handed.

In desperation as his lungs screamed for air, Daniels brought both hands up and slapped the Apache's ears as hard as he could. The Indian grunted in pain, and his grip on Daniels's throat loosened for an instant. Daniels heaved his body up off the ground, writhing like a horse trying to throw its rider. At the same time he slammed a punch into the Apache's stomach.

That did the trick. The man toppled off Daniels. Rolling quickly to the side, Daniels gasped for air, drawing huge lungfuls into his body. Bright stars and black circles were dancing in front of his eyes.

He heard another shot, then a bellow of rage. Getting his hands under him, Daniels pushed himself up onto his knees and looked around in time to see Buffalo Newcomb nearly take off an Apache's head with the knife he had found earlier. Blood spurted as the blade slashed across the Indian's throat.

The one whose arm he had broken was stunned. Daniels laced his fingers together and clubbed his fists across the Apache's jaw. That would keep him out of the fight for a while.

The fight, however, seemed to be over. At least, silence had fallen over the hillside. Daniels looked around, blinking back the sweat that dripped into his eyes, and took stock of the situation.

Buffalo was standing over the body of the brave he had just killed with his knife. Rafael peered around the corner of the adobe shack, his rifle in his hands. Scattered around the little clearing in front of the jacal were six Apaches, all of them dead except the one Daniels had just knocked out. Buffalo and Rafael had made their shots count, too; three of the bodies, including the Indian who had first attacked Daniels, had been felled by gunshot wounds. Daniels had accounted for two more, and Buffalo had taken care of the other man. Daniels stared at the corpses in amazement. He was damned lucky that he and his companions were not the ones who were dead.

With a swift, efficient motion, Buffalo leaned over and wiped the blood from his knife on the dead Apache's dark red shirt. He sheathed the blade, then turned and picked up the rifle he must have cast aside earlier after firing it. Opening the patch box on the stock, he took a cap and ball from the hollow and began to reload as he walked slowly toward Daniels.

"Reckon you must have dozed off," Buffalo said without looking at the young Texan. "Good thing you woke up when you did. I was round to the back, takin' care o' some business, when I heard the yellin' and shootin' start."

Daniels got to his feet as Buffalo reached him. "Sorry," he said. "I thought I wouldn't have any trouble staying awake."

"Well, don't fret about it overmuch. Don't seem to be any more of these bucks around right now. Ain't none of us hurt, and we got six dead Apaches that won't bother us no more."

"Five." Daniels nodded to the one whose arm he had broken. "This one's still alive, just knocked out."

One-handed, Buffalo pointed the rifle at the Indian's head, pulled back the hammer, and fired.

Daniels leaped in surprise, then turned away from the sight of what the musket ball had done to the Apache's face at close range. "What the hell!" he exclaimed.

"Six dead Apaches, like I said." Buffalo jerked a thumb toward the hut. "You'd best go see to the woman. Reckon she's prob'ly a mite scared."

Daniels swallowed and turned toward the jacal. Buffalo was right about one thing: Margarita was probably terrified, even though she wasn't screaming anymore.

He stopped just outside the doorway and looked back at Buffalo. "Did you have to do that?"

"Didn't figger it'd be a good idea to take him with us," Buffalo said. "And I sure as hell didn't intend to leave him alive to come after us later. I ain't stupid, boy.''

After a moment, Daniels nodded curtly. Buffalo's logic was harsh, but it made sense. Still, there should have been some other way. Killing a man in the heat of battle was one thing, but shooting him in cold blood like that, while he was unconscious . . .

He wondered what he would have done if Buffalo had not been there.

Trying not to think about the question, Daniels stepped into the hut. Margarita was sitting at the head of the bunk, her back against the wall of the shack, her shoulders hunched over slightly as she cradled the baby in her arms. Her eyes were huge and staring, but there was a flicker of recognition in them as Daniels came into the dim interior of the jacal.

''It's all right, Margarita,'' he said soothingly. ''Everything is fine.''

''The Apaches, they came back, no?''

He nodded. ''They did. But they're all dead now, and they won't bother you ever again.''

She looked down at his shirt and said anxiously, ''But you are hurt.''

Daniels had forgotten about the slash across the ribs. He glanced down and saw a fresh bloodstain, a thin line of red that ran across his side. Pulling up his shirt, he saw that the wound didn't amount to much. It was just a scratch, really, although it was starting to sting.

''I'll be fine,'' he told Margarita. ''Don't worry about me.''

She closed her eyes and her mouth began moving in a silent prayer. Daniels backed out of the hut, leaving her alone to collect herself.

Rafael was waiting for him. The Mexican nodded toward Buffalo, who was dragging the bodies of the Indians into a pile at the side of the little building. A tuneless whistle came from him as he worked. Stink had come out from wherever he had been hiding and was nosing around the bodies.

"Señor Buffalo is . . . an unusual man," Rafael said in a low voice. "You and I can never be friends, gringo, since you rode with the bandits who murdered my cousins, but at least you do not seem to take pleasure in killing."

"No. I'm not sure Newcomb does, either. He didn't sound like it."

"Ah, but did you see the look in his eyes? Mark my words, that one is a little crazy, señor."

Daniels frowned. Was Buffalo insane? Did the big man enjoy killing? He was good at it, that was for sure.

Buffalo pushed the possum away with a booted foot and said, "Get away from there, Stink. There's bound to be somethin' better around for you to eat than Injun."

Daniels and Rafael exchanged a glance, and Daniels shrugged. Even if Buffalo was mad, there was nothing they could do about it now.

Margarita came out of the hut a little later, carrying the baby. Her long dress brushed the dirt in front of the doorway as she walked. Daniels saw her look around nervously, as if she expected more Apaches to leap out at her. The bodies were out of sight around the corner of the jacal, and Daniels was glad for that. As much as the young woman had been forced to endure in the last twenty-four hours, the grisly spectacle of half a dozen dead Indians might have been too much for her.

Daniels hurried to her side and said, "Señora Salazar, these men are my companions, Buffalo Newcomb and Rafael Vasquez."

Gallantly, Rafael swept his sombrero off his head. "Rafael Sebastiano y Roderigo Vasquez," he said. "At your service, señora."

Buffalo contented himself with a nod. "Ma'am," he said curtly.

"I . . . think I remember you from last night, Señor Newcomb," Margarita said hesitantly. "You helped Señor Daniels deliver my baby, my little Antonia here."

Buffalo was starting to look uneasy again. He said

quickly, "Shoot, I didn't do much of anything. It was Daniels here who did all the work."

"And this morning you and Señor Vasquez fought off the Apaches." She summoned up a smile. "I am so happy the three of you found me here. My baby and I would have died without you."

That was probably true, Daniels thought. So some good had come out of everything.

Margarita's slender face became solemn again. "My husband," she said. "Where is he?"

"Well, señora," Daniels said uncomfortably, "you wouldn't have wanted to see him. We . . . we buried him already."

Margarita caught her bottom lip with her teeth, then went on after a moment, "*Sí*, I should probably thank you for that as well, señores. Please, I . . . I would like to see Alejandro's grave. I must pray for him to the Blessed Virgin."

"Sure." Daniels took her arm. "It's right around here."

Buffalo had had the sense to put the dead Indians on the other side of the hut from Salazar's grave. Daniels led Margarita to the spot. She looked at the small mound of earth for a moment, then turned and held out the baby to him. Surprised, Daniels hesitated slightly, then took the infant. While he cradled Antonia awkwardly in his arms, Margarita dropped to her knees, closed her eyes, crossed herself, and began to pray in a soft, almost inaudible voice.

Hearing the scrape of footsteps behind him, Daniels glanced over his shoulder and found Buffalo and Rafael watching him as he held the baby. Buffalo was grinning broadly, and even Rafael had a slight smile on his face. Daniels frowned. Maybe he did look a little silly standing there with a kid in his arms, but there was a proper time and place to be amused. This wasn't it.

After a few minutes, Margarita finished her prayers and stood up. She took the baby from Daniels, smiled in gratitude at him, and went with him to the front of the hut.

Buffalo pushed his hat to the back of his head and said, "Question now is, what're we goin' to do with you, ma'am?"

"This farm is my home, Señor Newcomb. Are you suggesting that I leave it?"

"You're going to have to," Daniels put in. "You can't stay out here, just you and the baby. It's too dangerous."

"The Indians who came this morning . . . do you think they were the same ones who . . . who killed Alejandro?"

Buffalo nodded. "I been thinkin' on that, ma'am, and I reckon there's a good chance it was the same braves, all right. I figger when they came here the first time and did for your husband, they heard you carryin' on inside—uh, with the baby about to come an' all, I mean—and they got spooked 'cause they knowed they hadn't done nothin' to you yet. Ain't nothin' an Injun's more leery of than crazy folks, and they might've thought you was crazy. Their curiosity must've got the best of 'em, though, so they come back this mornin' just to see what was really goin' on inside that hut."

Buffalo's theory made sense to Daniels. He added, "They were probably mighty surprised when they crept up here and found the three of us."

Rafael brought up the most practical question. "Is there a village or a mission anywhere near here, señora?"

"Sí, there is a mission two days' ride west of here, near the hills," Margarita said. "The padre, he comes sometimes to visit on his burro. The Indians do not bother him."

Daniels nodded. "That's where we'll take you, then. I'm sure the workers at the mission will take you in."

That seemed to be the best solution, and although she was a little hesitant about leaving the farm, Margarita agreed after a few minutes. She had to have realized there was no other way to protect herself and her baby, Daniels thought.

"You can ride with me," he said. "We'll get the mules loaded up and get out of here."

As Margarita went back into the hut to gather the few possessions she wanted to take with her, Buffalo ambled over to Daniels and said, "Good thing that mission's on our way. We already been slowed down enough."

"You mean if the mission hadn't been west of here, you wouldn't have taken her to it?"

"Guerrero's still got a big lead on us, boy," Buffalo pointed out. "I'd like to catch up to him 'fore he gets to that stronghold of his you heard about."

"Mighty anxious to settle the score with him, aren't you?"

"Ain't you?" Buffalo asked.

Not as much so as he had been back at the cantina, Daniels discovered as he thought over Buffalo's question. He was still angry with Guerrero for leaving him there, but on reflection, that might have been the best thing the *bandido* could have done for him. Leading the life of a robber had been eating away at Daniels's insides. Now he felt more human than he had in a long time.

But Guerrero was still holding those two girls captive, and Daniels knew he couldn't ride away from that. He had to do what he could to help them.

"I want to catch up to him," he said to Buffalo. "Let's leave it at that."

"Whatever you say, boy."

Less than a half hour later, they had the mules loaded and were mounted up. Well aware that more eyes might be watching them, even though one band of Apaches was dead, they left the jacal behind, riding west toward the mountains.

EIGHT

THE TALL, GRAY-HAIRED MAN in priest's robes came to the doorway of the church, the rope soles of his sandals making soft brushing sounds on the floor. He pushed open one of the heavy, ornately carved doors and looked out at the morning.

The priest's name was Father Vicente, and he had been the leader of the flock here at San Cristóbal for ten years. Ten good years, he thought often. The farmers who worshiped here were poor people when it came to money and property, but they were wealthy in spirit and love.

Father Vicente drew in a deep lungful of the cool, clean early morning air. Later, in just a very short time, the day would turn hot, but for now it was pleasant.

The mission of San Cristóbal sat at the edge of the plain, where the land began to slope up toward the foothills of the Sierra Madre. A creek that was born high in the mountains flowed down through the hills here, providing water for the mission before it slowed to a trickle that was soon swallowed up by the nearby desert. San Cristóbal was something of an oasis, surrounded by trees and green grass and productive fields. Father Vicente thought it was the prettiest place on earth, and he was thankful that the Lord had led him here to minister to the people of the foothills and the plains.

The padre started to turn away from the door when his sharp eyes spotted movement out on those plains. He stopped and waited, watching the figures that slowly moved out of the rising haze of heat and resolved themselves into a handful of riders on horseback.

Father Vincente frowned slightly, not recognizing any of the riders. There were seven or eight of them, more than he had thought at first. Some of them were riding double, however, even though there were a dozen or so extra mounts being led behind the men.

A noise behind him made the priest glance over his shoulder. One of the peasant boys who assisted him around the mission was sweeping in front of the altar. Father Vicente looked from the boy back to the strange riders. The man in the lead was close enough now for Father Vicente to see that he was dressed like a vaquero. There was a pistol holstered on the man's hip. Behind him rode five other men, all of them wearing the plain garb of farmers. The rifles they carried were not tools for working the land, however. On two of the horses, riding with the unshaven, rifle-carrying men, were young women.

Father Vicente looked behind him again, this time gazing at the golden candle holders which had graced the altar since the establishment of the mission nearly two hundred years earlier. "Juan," he called softly, and when the boy looked up, the priest flicked his hand toward the artifacts. "Take those and put them in the storeroom, behind the sacks of grain."

The boy frowned at him in puzzlement. "Padre . . . ?"

"Do as I say, lad," Father Vicente snapped, trying not to make his voice too harsh.

Juan nodded and put down his broom. The candle holders were heavy, but he carried them one at a time out a door at the rear of the sanctuary, which led to a storeroom.

The riders were entering the small yard in front of the church, Father Vicente saw as he turned his attention back to them. They were dusty and looked tired, as if they had been on the trail for a long time. The two women were the greatest puzzle; one of them wore a simple blouse and skirt and sandals, but the other's garb, despite the dust and dishevelment, bore the look of finery. There was elaborate stitching on her skirt, and Father Vicente saw lace at the throat and sleeves of her blouse. Both of the young women were very beautiful.

And both of them looked very frightened, as well.

The vaquero pulled his horse to a stop in front of the church. He had a lean, dark face and sat his saddle easily. He grinned at the priest and said, "*Buenos días*, padre. This is the mission of San Cristóbal, is it not?"

"That is right," Father Vicente admitted, stepping out of the church into the morning sunlight. "I am Father Vicente. Welcome."

"Thank you, Father." The man signaled for his men to dismount, then swung a leg over the back of his horse and dropped lightly to the ground. "I have heard much about this mission and its beauty and hospitality. I can see that the men who spoke to me of it did not lie. Such a pretty spot, here on the edge of nothing."

He was still smiling, but Father Vicente could see that the expression did not reach as far as his eyes. They were as cold as the wind from the mountains in the winter.

"What about the hospitality?" the man went on. "Was my friend speaking truly of that, as well?"

Father Vicente shrugged. "We have water and grain for your horses, and you are welcome to share our beans and tortillas, and to rest before you go on your way. What else would you have, my son?"

The man's grin widened. "I was told that you have many treasures here, padre. I would . . . look at them."

"Our only treasures are the sun and the land and the love of God," Father Vicente said, spreading his hands. "And those are free to everyone."

They were bandits, he was sure of that. He had seen their kind too many times before. They would take what they wanted and kill anyone who opposed them. He did not want bloodshed here at San Cristóbal. Nothing was worth such suffering.

"Ah, padre, you are being coy with me," the man said smugly. "I am Ignacio Guerrero, and you know why I am here."

Father Vicente's lips tightened. "I have heard men speak of you, Señor Guerrero. It is said that you are a thief, with the blood of many men on your hands."

Casually, Guerrero slipped his revolver out of its holster. "Truly it is spoken," he said, not aiming the gun at the priest but holding it so that it pointed in his general direction. "We need a meal and supplies and any gold and jewels that you have here, old man. I am going to the mountains to raise an army, and I will require much money."

"Another army," Father Vicente said with a sigh. "Will there never be an end to armies?"

"An end to killing, you mean?" Guerrero laughed shortly. "I pray not!" He jerked the gun barrel at Father Vicente. "Inside."

The priest glanced again at the two young women and could understand their fear now. If they were prisoners of a man like Guerrero, they would be suffering great torments.

Father Vicente led the way through the church. Guerrero came right behind him, followed by his men, a couple of whom prodded the women along. "The kitchen is through here," Father Vicente said, trying to keep his voice level and not show his own fear. If he could remain calm, there was a chance Guerrero would go about his godforsaken business and leave without harming anyone.

Guerrero's hand fell on his shoulder, halting him abruptly. "What about the treasures?" the bandit chief demanded.

Father Vicente started to turn around. "I told you, the only treasures—"

Suddenly, Guerrero slashed at him with the gun, raking the barrel alongside the priest's head. One of the women lifted her balled fist to her mouth and gasped. Father Vicente staggered, letting out an involuntary moan. He lifted his hand to his head and brought his fingers away, stained with the blood that leaked from the gash Guerrero's blow had opened.

"I do not want to hear your stupid platitudes, old man!" Guerrero told him savagely. "I know there are gold and jewels here, and I want them."

"This is a poor, humble mission," Father Vicente said between clenched teeth. The room spun dizzily around him. "We care nothing for worldly goods, for wealth—"

Again, Guerrero did not let him finish. He pulled back the hammer of the pistol and leveled it at Father Vicente's face. "I never saw a priest who cared nothing for wealth," he said scornfully. "Everyone knows the church is a bigger thief than any simple *bandido* such as myself. But I want my share, and I intend to have it." His voice hardened even more. "You will show me where to find the things I seek, or I will kill you and tear this mission down stone by stone until I find them. Or better still, I will find someone who is willing to show me. There are children here, and young women, no?"

Father Vicente felt his belly go cold. He knew that Guerrero would not hesitate to make good on his threat. Not only would he himself meet death, but his parishioners would then stand in danger of torture and murder as well. He had to prevent that.

"Very well," he grated. "I will show you. In the storeroom, there." He waved a hand toward the door.

Guerrero nodded to one of his men, who entered the storeroom quickly and came out in a matter of moments clutching the two candle holders. "This is all I found except some sacks of grain," he said disgustedly.

"That is all," Father Vicente spoke up before Guerrero could respond. "Those are the only artifacts we have. I swear it, señor."

Guerrero scowled. "That is all? No jeweled crucifix? No golden Madonnas?"

Father Vicente shook his head.

"Bah! You are too frightened to lie. You are a dog in the robes of a priest! I should kill you now."

The padre met Guerrero's angry gaze. "I am ready, if you so wish."

Guerrero took a deep breath. Gunning down a defenseless priest would not make him look any better in the eyes of his men, Father Vicente knew. He was counting on that, in fact.

After a moment, Guerrero let down the hammer of his gun and jammed it back in its holster. "Food!" he said. "We must have food."

"This way," Father Vicente said softly.

He took them to the kitchen. Three women were working there, and they all gasped and paled when they saw the bandits follow the priest into the big room. Father Vicente raised his hands and spoke quickly to calm them. "Do not be frightened," he said. "These men will have a meal, and then they will leave us in peace. Is that not true, Señor Guerrero?"

"We shall see," Guerrero snapped.

Under Father Vicente's direction, the women began preparing a meal of tortillas and beans and stew. While they were doing that, Guerrero dispatched three of his men to search the mission, just in case the priest had lied to him about not having any more treasures. Father Vicente winced as he heard the crash of overturned pews from the church.

The two prisoners huddled together in a corner with another of Guerrero's men watching them. Father Vicente glanced at them and saw the pleading expression in their eyes. They wanted him to help them somehow, to rescue them from what had to be a degrading captivity.

He doubted that it would do any good, but he decided he would have to speak to Guerrero about the matter. Lightly touching the dried blood on his scalp, the priest turned to Guerrero and said, "About those young women, señor . . ."

Guerrero grinned and inclined his head toward the prisoners. "Those *putas*, you mean?"

Neither of them looked like whores to Father Vicente. Certainly the better dressed of the two was not, and the other one possessed an innocence about her that belied Guerrero's ridiculous claim.

"Once you and your men have eaten and gathered your supplies, why not leave the women here at the mission?" the priest asked. "Once you reach the mountains, they will only slow you down."

Guerrero laughed, and Father Vicente did not like the sound of it. "Padre, if I did that, my own men would turn against me and probably shoot me. No, I cannot let that happen. Besides, the women are with us of their own free will." He looked at them. "Is that not so, señoritas?"

There was a moment of silence as Guerrero's question and his blatant lie hung in the air. Then one of the women, the one who wore fine clothes, jerkily nodded her head.

"Say it!" Guerrero commanded.

"*S-sí,*" the woman replied in a hoarse whisper. "We are . . . are with Señor Guerrero of our own free will—"

Her voice choked off, fear closing her throat.

Guerrero turned back to Father Vicente and shrugged expressively. "So you see, there is no reason to worry about them, padre. Worry about yourself instead. I have shot people for no other crime than being as poor as you seem to be."

Father Vicente did not doubt that brutal claim for an instant.

• • •

Despite her fear, Angelina Vasquez was all too aware of the hunger knotting her belly. Guerrero's men had not had time to steal very many supplies back at her parents' cantina, and during the days since that horrible afternoon, the group had been on short rations. She and Doña Isabella were given even less to eat than Guerrero's men, the bandit reasoning that since they were smaller, they did not require as much food.

The stew that was being prepared smelled wonderful. As she leaned back against the adobe wall of the kitchen, Angelina closed her eyes and breathed that delicious aroma. It was almost enough to make her forget all the terrible things that had happened to her. Almost . . .

But the long hours of terror and pain and degradation were always in the back of her mind. Guerrero had forced her into his bedroll the first night, then left her for the other men to use as they saw fit. He was keeping Isabella for himself, however, and he had made it clear that if any of the others tried to touch her, he would kill the man instantly. As far as Angelina knew, Guerrero had not yet molested Isabella, regardless of the things he said about them to the priest. In fact, Guerrero had even announced that he intended to marry the aristocratic young widow.

That might even happen, Angelina thought. As frightened as Isabella was, if this ordeal lasted much longer the girl might withdraw into herself, her brain refusing to work anymore. If that happened, she would go along with anything Guerrero said.

There were times when Angelina wished she could take that way out herself. But if she did, she would be denying herself the chance to obtain the thing that now meant more to her than anything else in the world.

Vengeance.

As soon as she had started to recover from the shock of seeing her mother and father killed, before she had even been assaulted by the bandits, she had vowed that she would someday kill Ignacio Guerrero.

To do that, she would have to remain sane. A retreat into madness would mean defeat.

She could not expect help from anyone. The only ones who might stand up to Guerrero would be *Juaristas* or the Imperial Army, and either group would merely turn her into another camp follower, even if they killed Guerrero. No, she was on her own, and she would have to bide her time, wait for the proper moment to strike. Killing Guerrero and escaping from his men would be difficult, but she would do it, sooner or later. . . .

Guerrero's sharp words and curt gestures brought her out of her reverie of vengeance. He was telling her and Isabella to serve the meal to him and the other men. Angelina moved without really thinking about it, following the bandit's orders.

She took a pot of stew from one of the mission women and carried it toward the table where Guerrero and his men sat. The ones he had sent to search the rest of the mission had returned, bearing the news that their quest had been futile. No other treasures had been found.

Angelina had to pass closely beside the priest as she brought the stew to the table. Her eyes met his for an instant, but she saw no hope there. It was obvious that he was going to do everything he could to keep Guerrero happy, in hopes of preventing any more violence in the mission.

She sat the pot of stew on the table. Isabella brought the tortillas, and one of the mission women carried the beans. Angelina's stomach growled, but she knew she would have to wait until the men were finished eating. Then, if there was any food left, she and Isabella would be permitted to have some of it.

The *bandidos* ate hungrily, indulging this appetite with the same enthusiasm they displayed in their others. Angelina and Isabella stood back to watch. The highborn young woman licked her lips greedily as her eyes followed the tortillas, with their scoops of beans and stew, into the mouths of the men. Angelina saw that and firmed her own resolve not to show her hunger.

When he was through, Guerrero stood up and stretched. He turned to the priest and said, "We have been riding since before dawn, and it would be nice to stay and rest for a while. But we must press on. I have an appointment to keep, an appointment with destiny. Show my men where your stores are kept, old man."

The priest nodded and went out, trailed by the bandits. Guerrero stayed behind to keep an eye on the two prisoners. He grinned at them and waved a hand toward the remains of the meal on the table. Isabella hurried over and began grabbing the scraps and stuffing them into her mouth. Angelina went more slowly, although it took an effort not to conduct herself as the other girl was doing.

Guerrero sauntered over to her and cupped her chin, lifting her head so that he could look into her eyes. "You are a stubborn one," he said, something almost like admiration in his voice. "You do not know what I mean when I speak of my destiny, do you?"

Angelina stared at him without answering. He had made several comments like that over the last day or so, but she had no idea what he was talking about.

"I would prefer that you were the widow of Don Hortensio," Guerrero went on. "The union would be much more enjoyable with you than with this spiritless cow."

Doña Isabella did not even glance at them.

Guerrero shrugged. "However, fate has placed this opportunity within my path, and I will not allow it to go by. Doña Isabella and I will be married, and her money added to the bounty my men and I shall reap will be the beginning of the empire I will build in the mountains." His breathing quickened as he spun his grandiose scheme. "I shall be the king of the Sierra Madre, and a king must have a suitable queen. The sluttish daughter of a rancher and cantina owner simply would not do, no matter how beautiful she is." He shook his head solemnly. "It is a pity."

He was mad, Angelina thought. In the middle of a country at war with itself, a land full of rebels and troops and savages, this minor *bandido* thought to make himself a power. A king, no less. Truly, Ignacio Guerrero was *loco*.

Angelina said nothing. She glanced at the table and saw that Isabella had already eaten most of the food that had been left. Guerrero shrugged and released her chin. Angelina took a deep breath and moved to the table, snatching a few morsels up before the other girl could get her hands on them.

Guerrero's men came back a few minutes later to report that they had loaded several bags full of supplies on the extra horses. The priest was with them, and he cast a troubled glance toward Angelina and Isabella as he stepped away from the bandits.

Guerrero jerked his head toward the door. "Bring the women," he told his followers. "We must ride."

One of the men grabbed Angelina's arm and pulled her along roughly. Another had hold of Isabella, but he handled her with a bit more gentleness, knowing that Guerrero valued her the more highly of the two prisoners. They were led out of the kitchen through a side door and along the church to the front of the building where the horses were tied and waiting.

As she was hustled onto one of the mounts and a bandit swung up behind her—taking advantage of the opportunity to press his arm against her breasts as he settled into the saddle—Angelina saw that the priest had trailed them out. His lips were moving in a prayer. He was the only one who had the courage to venture out after Guerrero. Angelina glanced around the mission and saw faces peering out of windows, frightened faces of people who knew the kind of man Guerrero was.

Guerrero mounted up and turned his horse to face the priest before he left. "I wish you had had more treasures, old man," he sighed. "What kind of mission is this, anyway?"

"I fear you would not understand, señor," the priest answered softly. "But I pray that God will take away the evil that you have in your heart."

Guerrero laughed harshly. "When I am the king of

these lands, you will bow down to me, priest, and not to God.''

The man in the robe shook his head, finally pushed into disagreeing with the bandit.

''Oh, ho, you think not?'' Guerrero's gun appeared in his hand. The pistol crashed. The priest lurched forward, grimacing and clutching at a bullet-torn leg. Guerrero holstered his gun and said, ''You can start now, old man. Bow down to me, Ignacio Guerrero.''

The priest's balance deserted him. The injured leg folded up beneath him, throwing him forward onto his face.

''You see?'' Guerrero demanded. ''Even priests know their real lord and master.''

He wheeled his horse and galloped away from the church, his men trailing after him.

Angelina looked over her shoulder and saw the wounded priest writhing in the dirt. Even now, he would probably preach forgiveness.

But as far as Angelina was concerned, it would be a good day indeed when Ignacio Guerrero died.

NINE

BUFFALO WAS CONVINCED THAT they were still being watched, but Daniels couldn't see any sign of it. When he asked himself if he wanted to trust his own eyesight over Buffalo's instinct, he was unsure what the answer was.

Having Margarita and the baby along did not slow them down as much as he had expected it might. She was not a complainer, and little Antonia slept in her mother's arms most of the time. Daniels's mule was sturdy and didn't seem to mind carrying double.

As they rode, Margarita told him a little about her life. She had grown up in a small village to the south, and nothing remarkable had ever happened to her. She had married Alejandro Salazar, who was ten years her senior, because she had many brothers and sisters and her father was anxious to have one less mouth to feed. But Alejandro had proven to be a good man, and though she had not loved him at first, the marriage had been quite satisfactory to her. Alejandro had treated her well, and she had grown to care very deeply for him. But he had had the idea that he wanted to have his own farm, rather than working the land that his family had owned, and so he had taken his bride and gone in search of his own place.

Daniels knew how tragically that search had ended. And yet he wasn't the one to say that Alejandro Salazar had been wrong, he decided. Maybe the man had been foolish to come out here with his young wife, but Daniels couldn't fault him for wanting a place to call his own. A similar desire had led him from east Texas to the Rio Grande country.

After she had talked for quite a while, Margarita turned her head to look at him and said, "But you have told me nothing of yourself, Señor Daniels. How do you come to be in my poor country?"

The question sent Daniels's mind back to his own home, the one he had made with Willa and Callie and Matt. He took a deep breath, feeling the old familiar pain at the base of his chest. "I'm not really sure how I got here," he replied. "Things change, and you never know why."

Margarita frowned. She didn't understand his answer, he thought. But then, he didn't, either.

"What about you, Señor Buffalo?" she asked, looking over at the big man. "Why are you here in Mexico? You are a Texan like Señor Daniels, are you not?"

Buffalo grinned. "Well, now, I was born in Texas, but I like to think of myself as sort of a citizen of the whole West," he said. "Reckon I've seen durn near all of it, from Mexico to Canada and all the way to California. Been shot at in just about ever' place I've visited, too. For some reason, folks just don't always take kindly to me. You take the time me'n Stink was up along the Oregon trail with that Parkman feller. We was stayin' in a Crow village whilst Parkman parleyed with the chief. He was a writer, you know—Parkman, not that Crow chief—and he was gatherin' stories to go in some book. Now, I never really seen the point in books myself, but Parkman was payin' good money for guides. So I went with him and we stopped with them Crows and one of th' braves got his feathers in an uproar 'cause he said I was messin' with his squaw. Well, I weren't doin' no such thing, o' course. Now, her sister, mind you, that was diff'rent. . . . But, hell, I was talkin' 'bout that brave who figgered he was goin' to scalp me or some such nonsense, and Parkman, shoot, he seemed to think that the feller was right, and there I was, workin' for him—Parkman, that is, not the brave. I wouldn't work for no savage like that, no matter how much money he offered me. . . . Well, I guess he could've come up with enough money, 'cept whoever seen a Injun with money, they ain't got no use for it. Which is why a white man won't never really be able to understand a Injun, 'cause there's nothin' more important to most white men than money. Not me, o' course. Money ain't good for nothin' by itself, it's what you can buy with it, like good whiskey or a pretty gal—Ow! Dammit, Stink, you bit me!''

Thank God, Daniels thought silently. Somebody needed to.

Buffalo sucked on his possum-bit finger for a moment, then said, "Now where was I? Oh, yeah, up on the Oregon Trail . . .''

Margarita had said the mission was two days' ride to the west. As they made camp that night, Daniels hoped that they would reach the place before dark the next day. If they did, they might be able to spend the night there, he thought. It would be good to eat something besides jerky, maybe even sleep indoors for a change.

Rafael was the only one of the group who had a real bedroll, and he didn't offer it to Margarita until Daniels had given him a hard look and suggested that such an offer would be a nice gesture. Then the Mexican sighed, spread his blankets, and stepped back with a wave of his hand. "Please, señora, with my compliments.''

"*Gracias*, Señor Vasquez.'' Margarita had already nursed the baby again, retreating behind a scrubby bush to do so. She crawled into the blankets and snuggled down with Antonia. Daniels thought she was more exhausted than she was willing to admit.

Their supper had consisted of jerky again, washed down with canteen water. His teeth ached from chewing the stuff. It had been so long since he had had coffee, he had almost forgotten what it tasted like. Things would be different when they reached the mission, though. There they could have hot food, real food, and coffee, too. The mission was called San Cristóbal, Margarita had said during one of the lulls in Buffalo's rambling monologue.

As far as Daniels could tell, Buffalo never had reached the end of the story about what had happened to him in the Crow village. Daniels wasn't about to ask him to finish it, either.

He walked over to where the big man was sitting cross-legged in the dirt. Buffalo's hand was up somewhere under his poncho, scratching at flea bites. "Damn little vermin," he muttered. "Ain't nothin' worse'n a flea bite, less'n it's chiggers. I've had chiggers so bad I was minded to douse myself in kerosene and set the stuff on fire, just to roast the little bastards."

"Wouldn't that roast you, too?" Daniels asked, hunkering on his heels.

"Never was able to work out that part of it. But it'd sure as hell get rid of them chiggers."

Daniels couldn't argue with that. He said, "You think we'll get to that mission tomorrow?"

"More'n likely, if the Comanches don't slow us down too much."

Daniels frowned. "Comanches?"

"I told you, they been watchin' us all day."

"I never saw any sign of them."

Buffalo snorted and said, "You wouldn't, boy, you wouldn't."

"Why would they hang back and watch us? If they're out there, why don't they just jump us and get it over with?"

"Like I said before, Injuns is just naturally curious. They're prob'ly tryin' to figger out what a gal and a baby, a Mexican, a gringo in Mex clothes, and a fine specimen o' manhood like ol' Buffalo're doin' out here by our lonesome. Reckon they'll study on that for a while, then decide to come ask us. Could be they'll get around to that tomorrow.''

"Why tomorrow?'' Daniels asked, assuming that there were even any Indians nearby. "According to you, they've been following us since before we found that hut yesterday.''

"They probably knew those Apaches was around. Now, a Comanche ain't afraid of Apaches, no, sir, but a Comanch' ain't a damn fool, neither. They let us take care of those 'Paches for 'em.'' Buffalo shrugged. "As for why they'll make their move tomorrow, I can't tell you, son. But my gut says they could, and I've learned to trust that feelin' over the years. It's kept me alive a time or two.''

"Well, I guess we'll see. We'd better keep a good watch tonight. I won't doze off again.''

"That'd be a right good idea,'' Buffalo said.

They followed their usual routine, Rafael standing first watch, followed by Buffalo and then Daniels. When Buffalo woke him to stand his turn, Daniels shivered at the cold that had permeated the landscape during the night. He hoped that Margarita and Antonia were warm enough in the blankets.

Along toward dawn, the baby woke up, squalling briefly before Margarita roused and began to nurse her. Daniels felt uncomfortable again as he heard the sucking, but the sound of Margarita's voice, little more than a whisper as she spoke tenderly to the infant, took away some of the chill in the air for him. That was a good sound, a mother talking to her baby.

The sun came up, Daniels having no trouble staying awake until dawn this time, and he woke the others as daylight washed over the plains. After a cold breakfast, they hit the trail again, heading west with only minor detours to negotiate more gullies.

The terrain became a little rougher as the morning passed. There were just as many arroyos as before, but now the land in between the dry washes was more rolling than before, almost hilly in spots. It was still arid,

though. Long miles remained before they would reach
the foothills and the occasional streams that brought life
to the land.

Buffalo glanced around, eyes narrowed, and Daniels
knew he was looking for Comanches. For the sake of
all of them, he hoped that Buffalo's instincts would be
wrong this once.

When midday came and went, Daniels began to think
that maybe they had a chance to reach the mission without any more trouble. Margarita had been to the place
several times and was starting to recognize landmarks.
"We have made good time," she said. "We should be
there by late afternoon."

"That's good," Daniels replied. "I'm looking forward to seeing some more folks again—"

"Don't reckon this's what you had in mind," Buffalo
cut in, "but look up ahead, son."

Rafael caught his breath, the air hissing sharply between his teeth as he spotted the figures appearing from
an arroyo up ahead. "Is that—"

"It sure as hell is," Buffalo said. "Comanches, just
like I thought."

Daniels wasn't going to waste his breath congratulat-
ing Buffalo on being right. His pulse was starting to thud
in his chest, and his hand tightened on the rifle he held.
They had armed themselves with knives taken off the
dead Apaches back at the hut, but the three rifles were
still the only guns they had. That wasn't much firepower
to drive off a dozen or more Comanches.

And there were that many, sitting on their horses,
waiting for the little group that had been foolish enough
to travel across this desolate land.

Buffalo said quietly, "I know a young feller back in
Texas who's mighty good with a Henry rifle, and his pa
handles a Colt better'n any man I ever seen. Wish the
two o' them was here right now."

"We could use the extra guns, all right," Daniels
breathed.

Buffalo snorted. "Hell, that ain't what I mean at all.

Just figgered they'd enjoy watchin' me deal with these
Comanch', that's all.''

With that, he urged his horse into a trot, pulling ahead
of the others. Daniels glanced over at Rafael. The Mexican shrugged, as if to say that if Buffalo was crazy
enough to meet the Indians that much sooner, then let
him.

Buffalo reined in when he was about twenty feet from
the Indians, who were watching him expressionlessly.
He raised his right hand in the universal symbol of greet-
ing and boomed out in Spanish, "Howdy, boys!"

Even though Daniels couldn't see Buffalo's face from
his vantage point, he would have been willing to bet that
there was a big grin on the bearded visage.

Daniels and Rafael pulled their mounts to a stop
twenty feet behind Buffalo, putting the big man halfway
between them and the Indians. One of the Comanches
grunted something in his native tongue. Daniels knew
only a few words of Comanche and couldn't make out
what the brave was saying, but then the Comanche
switched to Spanish, asking, "Why are you here, white
man?"

Without taking his eyes off the Indians, Buffalo
waved his free hand at his companions and replied, "My
pards and I are headin' for the mission at San Cristóbal.
That gal there's got a little 'un, a newborn babe, and we
figgered she'd be better off at the mission."

"You are her man?" the Comanche asked.

Buffalo shook his head. "None of us are. Her man
got hisself killed by Apaches."

Daniels felt a shiver go through Margarita at Buffalo's
words. She was already trembling slightly, just from the
presence of the Indians. Little Antonia fretted quietly in
her blankets.

The Comanche who seemed to be the spokesman nodded. "The Apaches are bad. That is why my people have
made war on them and driven them from the land called
Texas."

That was something, Daniels thought, a Comanche—

one of the most bloodthirsty lot of savages anybody had ever seen—talking about how bad the Apaches were. The Comanches had chased the Apaches across the border into Mexico because they wanted Texas to themselves, to raid as they wished. And now the Comanches were extending their warlike ways on down into Mexico.

The leader of the band was still speaking. "What happened to these Apaches?"

"We killed 'em," Buffalo declared flatly. "Ever' damn one of them."

If these were the same Comanches who had been following them, they probably already knew about that. Daniels figured that the group had passed them during the night, while he and the others were camped, riding ahead to set up this trap.

Because trap was the right word for it. He looked to right and left and saw no cover anywhere, just flat, dusty land sparsely dotted by a few little bushes. They had passed another arroyo about a mile back, but that was too far away to do them any good. There was no way they could outrun those Comanches' ponies for a mile. And the Indians had the way ahead blocked.

The leader nodded solemnly. "It is good that you killed those Apache dogs," he said to Buffalo. "You have saved us the trouble. For that we are grateful. We would trade with you."

Daniels felt a surge of hope. Indians were unpredictable, but if they could work some sort of trade with these Comanches, there was at least a chance that they would be allowed to ride on.

Buffalo nodded. "We'd be right honored to trade with you, chief. What you need? We got tobacco and a little jerky—"

"What about whiskey?" the man cut in sharply.

"Sorry. Nary a drop," Buffalo said with a shake of his head. "We don't even have any tequila. I was fixin' to ask you if you had any we could trade you out of."

One of the Indians suddenly walked his horse forward

a few steps. Like the others, he was dressed in buckskin leggings and a beaded shirt, but his powerful frame stretched the garments. Without a doubt, he was the biggest Indian Daniels had ever seen. He held a long, sharp lance across the back of his horse, and he looked cruel enough to use it.

Buffalo sat in his saddle without moving as the Comanche approached. The leader of the group spoke a few curt words to the big brave, who replied with a grunt. He drew rein when he was less than six feet from Buffalo.

The Comanche lifted the lance, and for a moment, Daniels thought he intended to plunge it into Buffalo's chest. Daniels's impulse was to lift his rifle and fire it at the Indian. At this range, he would have trouble missing as big a target as the brave presented. But that would bring the rest of the Indians down on them, and there was no doubt they would be massacred. Besides, Buffalo was sitting stock-still, seemingly not worried.

Turning the tip of the lance toward Buffalo, the Comanche urged his pony forward another step. He reached out with the lance and prodded lightly at the bag hanging from Buffalo's saddle horn. Stink hissed and twisted, bringing his snout within range of the lance. The possum bit furiously at the weapon.

Surprised, the big Comanche jerked back the lance. He glowered at the bag containing the possum and spoke quickly.

"Our brother Tall Moon says you have an evil spirit in your pouch," the leader began to translate into Spanish. He sounded amused, and there were smiles on the faces of some of the other Comanches. "Tall Moon says that he must kill it, otherwise his lance will be cursed with bad medicine from the thing's bite."

"I know what he's sayin'," Buffalo replied. "And it's too damn bad. That ain't no evil spirit; it's a possum. Though I reckon there sometimes ain't much diff'rence 'twixt the two. But it don't matter. Evil spirit or not, what's in the bag is mine, and Tall Moon ain't to mess with it.''

Tall Moon must have understood enough of Buffalo's daring statement to follow its meaning, because his scowl darkened. Daniels's nerves were about as tight as they could get already, and he felt them trying to pull even more taut.

"We have offered to trade with you, white man," the spokesman for the Comanche said. "Why do we not trade for what is in that pouch?"

"Ain't sayin' I'd consider it, but what've you got to give me in return for ol' Stink here?"

"Your lives," the Indian said.

"Señor Buffalo," Rafael put in quickly, "if all they want is the possum—"

"Shut up, Rafe!" Buffalo said. "This is between me and this feller here." He gestured at Tall Moon, who was waiting with the angry glower still on his face.

"You refuse to trade?" the leader asked.

"Didn't say that," Buffalo replied. "But it seems to me you fellers'd be gettin' the worst of the deal. We'd get to ride on without bein' bothered, and all you'd have to show for it'd be a mangy ol' possum. He's mean, at that, and he's too damn stringy to make a good pot o' stew." Moving slowly so that the gesture wouldn't be misinterpreted, Buffalo lifted his hand and scratched at his beard, evidently in deep thought. "Let's see, ought to be somethin' we could work out. . . . Say, how 'bout if I fight this here Tall Moon feller?"

"You would challenge our brother?" The Comanche sounded surprised.

"Sure. Winner gets the possum and gets to ride on with his friends."

"You sound as if you intend to win."

"No point in it otherwise, now, is there?"

The leader spoke to Tall Moon in Comanche for a moment, and then the massive Indian nodded eagerly. What passed for a smile touched his face.

"Very well," the spokesman told Buffalo. "Tall

Moon has agreed to accept your challenge. He says you will fight with knives.''

"Fair enough," Buffalo said. "I'll get ready."

He turned his horse and rode slowly back to the others. In a low voice, Daniels said, "I heard what you're planning to do, Buffalo. You can't fight that Indian! Now that we're together again, we'd better try to make a run for it—"

"And run where?" Buffalo cut in. "Shoot, we'd have arrows stickin' out all over us 'fore we got a hundred yards, and you know it."

"But why not give them the animal?" Rafael argued again. "Surely you do not value it over our lives!"

"Me'n Stink been together a long time." Buffalo sighed. "But I reckon I'd give him up if'n I thought it'd do any good. It won't, though. Them bucks see they got us scared, they won't stop with askin' for no possum. They'll want the gal next, and then our mules, and then they're liable to kill us just for the fun of it. Nope, we got to make 'em respect us, and I don't see but one way of doin' that—by beatin' their biggest man."

"But what if that Tall Moon kills you instead?" Daniels asked.

"I'm dependin' on you to see that he don't," Buffalo said. "If it looks like he's about to do me in, shoot the son of a bitch, then take off a-runnin'. I'll keep the others busy and give you as much start as I can."

"They'll kill you for sure then."

Buffalo grinned. "Yep, but at least that big jigger won't get the pleasure of doin' it. You put a ball through his head 'fore you let him finish me off, you hear."

Daniels swallowed and nodded. "I hear."

Buffalo dismounted, took off his hat, and hung it on the saddle horn along with Stink's bag. He handed his rifle to Daniels, then his poncho followed, revealing his butternut shirt and suspenders. He draped the poncho over the saddle. The knife he had taken from one of the dead Apaches was in his boot. He bent over and slid it out. "Wish I had my Arkansas Toothpick," he grunted. "Reckon this'll have to do, though."

With that, he turned and stalked toward the Indians.

TEN

TALL MOON WAS WAITING for him. The Indian had stripped his shirt off, leaving his chest bare. He held a rope-handled knife in his right hand. His face wore a fierce expression as Buffalo approached, no doubt calculated to throw fear into his white opponent.

He was wasting his time with Buffalo Newcomb, Daniels thought. There was probably nothing short of another woman giving birth that could scare Buffalo.

They were all going to die here, Daniels was sure of that. Even if Buffalo could defeat Tall Moon, the other Comanches would fall on them and kill them. But at least they could die with some measure of respect. And there was a good chance the Indians wouldn't hurt Margaret and Antonia, but rather take the two with them, adopt them into the tribe. It would be a harsh life, but better than dying.

Daniels hoped it would be so.

"Señor Buffalo, he will win, *sí?*" Margarita asked, her voice trembling slightly.

"Of course he will," Daniels replied, forcing his own voice to sound heartier than he felt. He looked over at Rafael, saw the pallor on the Mexican's face, and knew that Rafael understood the situation as well as he did.

Buffalo stopped a few feet away from Tall Moon,

gripping his own knife and smiling at his opponent. In English, he said, "Ready to die, you red-skinned heathen?"

It had been a long time since Daniels had heard his own language, so long that for a moment he had trouble believing his ears. Evidently, Tall Moon didn't understand a word of Buffalo's brash question, but he must have caught the meaning of it from the sound of the words. He grunted again, then suddenly leaped forward, swinging the knife at Buffalo's head.

Buffalo dropped down and to the side, but the blow was only a feint. Tall Moon changed direction with his knife, moving almost too fast for Daniels to follow what he was doing, and thrust the point of it at Buffalo's throat.

But Buffalo was gone again, darting nimbly aside and bringing up his own blade in a sweeping slash. Tall Moon had to pull his arm up and back to avoid having it hacked open. That left his midsection unprotected. Buffalo wasn't in position to strike with his knife, but he was able to kick Tall Moon in the belly. The Indian staggered back as a cry of appreciation for Buffalo's tactics came from the other members of the band.

Pressing his advantage, Buffalo lunged forward, jabbing the knife at Tall Moon. The Comanche knocked the blow aside with his left arm and slashed at Buffalo. The big man from Texas was a fraction of a second too slow in getting out of the way, and Tall Moon's blade raked across Buffalo's cheek, leaving a thin line of red that disappeared into the tangle of his beard.

A second cry went up from the other Comanches. Their warrior had drawn first blood.

Buffalo backed off, lifting his free hand to his face and touching the wound. He wiped off several drops of blood, then gave Tall Moon another grin and licked the drops of crimson from his fingers. With a screech like that of a panther, Buffalo leaped at the Indian, flailing crazily with the knife.

"He is mad!" Rafael exclaimed.

Tall Moon must have thought the same thing. Disconcerted by Buffalo's actions, the Comanche fell back before the attack, giving ground for several feet. The two blades rang together again and again as Tall Moon parried Buffalo's blows. Then he borrowed a trick from his enemy and launched a kick, aiming his moccasined foot at Buffalo's groin.

Buffalo's left arm whipped around, the fingers catching Tall Moon's ankle and yanking savagely. The Comanche came off his feet, flying through the air to land heavily on his back. Buffalo threw himself after Tall Moon, trying to land on top of him and bring this deadly contest to an end.

Even shaken up by the impact of his landing, Tall Moon was able to roll desperately to the side. Buffalo hit the ground instead. Tall Moon slashed at him, but Buffalo twisted and caught the Comanche's wrist before the blow could land. His own thrust was stopped by Tall Moon's left hand grasping his wrist.

Locked together that way, the two men began to roll over and over in the dirt, raising such a cloud of dust around themselves that the spectators, white, Mexican, and Indian alike, could barely see what was going on. Margarita was pressed up against Daniels, and his heart was pounding so strongly inside his chest that it seemed as if it ought to knock her from the saddle. He had a rifle in each hand and wished that he could drop one of the weapons to put a reassuring arm around her, but he didn't dare. He might need both of the rifles in a few minutes.

Buffalo was on top, then underneath, then on top again. But always Tall Moon was gripping his wrist so that he could not plunge the blade down. Likewise, Buffalo held on for dear life to the Indian's knife arm. The battle was fought in an eerie near silence, broken only by the grunts of the combatants and the occasional stomp of a hoof from a nervous horse. There were no more cheers from the other Comanches. The battle had gone too far for that.

The next exclamation would probably be a death rattle.

Daniels leaned forward in the saddle, pressing against Margarita, his breath hissing between his teeth. Buffalo had wound up on the bottom again, and the two men stayed that way for long seconds, long enough for the wind to shred the cloud of dust surrounding them and start to blow it away. Daniels could see more clearly now, and he could see the muscles bulging on Tall Moon's arms and shoulders as he forced his knife inexorably toward Buffalo's throat. It seemed he was on the verge of victory.

Buffalo pulled a knee up and jammed it into Tall Moon's side. The Comanche grunted and twisted away from the blow, but that gave Buffalo enough room to plant his foot in the Indian's belly. He heaved with both arms as he kicked out, and suddenly Tall Moon was sailing over Buffalo's head to go crashing into the ground headfirst.

Buffalo rolled over and came up on hands and knees, lunging after Tall Moon. His knife swiped down, ripping across the Comanche's right forearm, severing muscles and tendons. Tall Moon screamed involuntarily as his fingers stopped working and the knife slipped away from him. Buffalo smashed his free arm into the Indian's throat, pinning him to the ground as he lay half on top of him. He drove Tall Moon's chin up, stretching his throat in readiness for the final blow, the slash that would end the fight—and the Comanche's life.

Buffalo brought the blade to a halt when it was barely touching the taut skin of Tall Moon's throat. He looked up, blinking back sweat from his eyes, and called to the leader of the Comanches, "Well?"

Amazingly, Daniels thought he saw a hint of a smile play across the Indian's face as he regarded the scene before him. There was some muttering from the other warriors, but the leader stopped that with a quick word. To Buffalo, he said, "You fight very well. I am surprised you stopped and did not kill Tall Moon, as you killed the Apache when he was helpless.''

So Buffalo had been right, Daniels thought fleetingly. The Comanches *had* been watching during the fight at the hut. They had seen Buffalo shoot the unconscious Apache. No wonder they expected him to kill Tall Moon.

But Buffalo Newcomb was usually full of surprises, as Daniels was coming to find out. Tall Moon lay still, the knife against his throat, as Buffalo said, ''The Apaches are lying dogs. If one gave me his word not to follow me and ambush me again, I wouldn't believe him. But if a Comanche told me the same thing, I'd know he was speakin' the truth.''

''You want such a pledge from me, white man, after you have crippled one of my best warriors? Tall Moon will never be able to use that arm properly again.''

''I figger that's better'n dyin'.'' Buffalo grinned down at the defeated Comanche beneath him. ''Besides, I'm bettin' that ol' Tall Moon here'll figger out some other way to kill folks just as good with his left hand, don't you?''

This time there was definitely a smile on the leader's face. He lifted a hand, palm out, and said, ''Very well. You have my word, as we agreed. You may keep your . . . evil spirit, and you and your friends will have safe passage to your destination. Beyond that, though, I make no promises. Now, release our brother.''

Buffalo pulled the knife away from Tall Moon's throat, rolling to the side and standing up quickly in case the Indian tried to resume the battle. That didn't seem likely, considering the wound Tall Moon had suffered, but Buffalo was taking no chances.

A couple of the other braves rode forward and swung down to help Tall Moon to his feet. With a hatred-filled glare directed toward Buffalo, the big Indian allowed himself to be assisted back to his horse.

When Tall Moon was mounted, the spokesman for the group lifted his hand to Buffalo again, then wheeled his horse and galloped toward the arroyo where they had

lain in wait. The others followed, disappearing from
sight in a matter of seconds. Daniels watched them go,
then heaved a sigh of relief, hardly able to believe that
they were all still alive.

Buffalo slid the knife back into his boot and walked
slowly toward his companions, slapping some of the
dust from his shirt. The cut on his cheek had crusted
over already. When he reached his horse, he poked a
blunt finger against the bag holding the possum and said,
"If I ain't the biggest damn fool there ever was, fightin'
that big ol' Injun just to keep him from scalpin' you,
you ungrateful little varmint."

Daniels grinned down at him. "Stink may not be
grateful, Buffalo, but the rest of us are."

"*Sí*, Señor Buffalo," Rafael said. "I was convinced
that we were all going to die. But you were magnifi-
cent!"

Buffalo dropped the poncho over his head, then
picked up his hat. "See that you remember that, son,"
he said as he swung up into the saddle. "We'd best get
movin' if we want to get to that mission 'fore dark."

"You're sure the Comanches won't bother us again?"
Daniels asked.

"As sure as you can ever be about Injuns," Buffalo
shrugged. "That chief struck me as a honorable feller.
He'll keep his word, and he'll make Tall Moon and the
others leave us alone, too. Still, I'd like to get behind
some nice thick walls, just so's we don't tempt 'em too
much."

That sounded good to Daniels, too. With Buffalo leading the way, the four of them rode on toward San Cristóbal.

The sun was still about an hour above the horizon when
the little party topped a rise and came within sight of
the mission. They had not been bothered by the Comanches or by any other Indians. Daniels heaved a sigh of
relief and, without thinking, tightened the arm that was

around Margarita. She said, "Yes, señor, that is San Cristóbal. You will stay there?"

The question took Daniels by surprise. He had assumed that she knew he and Buffalo and Rafael would be riding on once they had delivered her to the mission and maybe rested there overnight. Keeping his tone gentle, he said, "I wish we could, señora, but we have business in the mountains. Maybe we could stop there again when we're done with our chore."

"That would be good." Margarita's voice was solemn. "When my daughter is older, I would like for her to meet the three men who helped give her life . . . especially you, Señor Daniels."

Embarrassed and unsure how to reply, Daniels kept riding. He saw Buffalo and Rafael both glance over at him and grin, and he knew they had overheard the exchange.

"We'd best keep our eyes open," he said gruffly. "Wouldn't want to get this close to the mission and then have those Indians jump us again."

"Them Comanches are long gone, and there ain't no other Injuns around right now," Buffalo declared, still smiling.

"You sound mighty sure of that."

"I was right about the Comanch', weren't I?"

Daniels couldn't argue with that. He said, "Let's get on down there anyway."

It was a pretty place, Daniels saw as they approached. A stream that came out of the foothills provided water for the fields. The mission itself consisted of a large church with an arched entrance and a cross atop its bell tower, plus several smaller connected buildings, all of adobe with red shingled roofs. In addition, there were quite a few huts visible that would house the peasants who worked in the fields and tended the mission's livestock. Altogether, a couple of hundred people might live here, and surely among that number was someone who would take Margarita and Antonia in and give them a home.

Dogs began to bark as the riders entered the plaza in front of the church's entrance, trailed by the pack mules. Buffalo reined in, casting his eyes around as the others halted behind him. After a moment, the big man turned his head and said to Daniels, "Notice anything a mite funny, son?"

Daniels frowned. "I don't think so. Looks like a nice place— Wait a minute. There's nobody around."

Buffalo flipped a hand toward the dogs, which stayed a good distance away from the newcomers to do their carrying on, and said, "That's right. It's gettin' late, but there still ought to be folks in the fields. An' where's the padre?"

One of the heavy double doors of the church suddenly began to open with a squeal of hinges. Daniels said, "Maybe this is him now."

The door stopped when the crack was only a few inches wide, and the barrel of a rifle was thrust through it. "Do not move, señores!" a harsh voice commanded.

"Don't reckon that's the padre," Buffalo said dryly. Not sounding overly concerned, he went on, "Best do as the feller says 'til we find out what's goin' on around here."

The door opened a little wider and a man stepped out holding the rifle. He was dressed much like Daniels, in the white shirt and pants of a laborer. The gun in his hands was an ancient flintlock, the kind called a sna-phaunce. The muzzle trembled a little as he kept it trained on them.

"If you are bandits, you will find no more plunder here," the man said. "Your friends have already taken everything."

"We ain't bandits, mister," Buffalo rumbled in reply, "and if you folks have had trouble, it weren't any of our doin'. Fact of the matter is, we're lookin' for a bunch of *bandidos* ourselves."

Margarita spoke up. "Please, señor," she said to the man with the rifle, "these men are good. They mean no harm. You remember me, Margarita Salazar."

The Mexican frowned at her over the sights of the flintlock. "Señora Salazar? From the farm east of here?"

Margarita nodded.

"*Sí*, I remember you, señora. Where is your husband?"

"Dead," Margarita answered bleakly. "The Apaches killed him. They would have killed me, as well, and my baby, if these men had not saved our lives."

"Baby?"

Margarita held up Antonia, wrapped in her blankets. "My daughter," she said proudly.

The man lowered the rifle slightly. "And you say these strangers helped you, señora?"

"*Sí*. Could we get down, señor? We have ridden many long hours and are all tired."

He nodded, lowered the flintlock some more, and took one hand off it to motion them to dismount. Then he waved to one side, and several more men came around the corner of the church. Two of them carried pitchforks, and the others had machetes.

"San Cristóbal has had great troubles, señores," he said stiffly to Buffalo, Daniels, and Rafael. "You will forgive us for being careful."

"No need for forgivin', friend," Buffalo said as he swung down from the saddle. "Reckon we understand how come you to be a mite skittish. You say bandits hit you?"

"*Sí*," the man nodded. "Two days ago. They stole our grain and other provisions, and the padre, he was wounded."

"Do you know who those bandits were?" Daniels asked, figuring that he already knew the answer.

The man's head bobbed up and down again. "The leader spoke his name with great pride. It was Ignacio Guerrero."

"That don't come as no surprise," Buffalo said. "That's the skunk we're trailin', all right. Him and his men made good time. 'Course, we got slowed up a mite, too."

"Did Guerrero have two women with him?" Rafael asked.

"I was not here when the outrage occurred, señor, but I have heard that there were women with him. Father Vicente can tell you."

"Reckon we'll be pretty anxious to talk with him," Buffalo said.

"Come with me. I will take you to him."

The man said nothing else as they followed him through the church to the priest's quarters in the rear of the mission. Several of the machete-carrying peasants trailed along behind them, just in case this was some sort of trick. As they walked through the sanctuary, their footsteps echoing hollowly against the high ceiling, Daniels tried to remember the last occasion when he had been in a church.

It had been a long time. Back when Willa and Matt were still alive . . .

They left the church through a rear door, emerging onto a covered walkway that led them alongside a low adobe annex. There were several doors into the building, and the man took them to the second one. "Father Vicente is still weak from his wound," he warned them. "You must not tire him overmuch."

"We'll try not to," Daniels said.

When the man opened the door and stepped aside to let them in, they entered a small, shadowy chamber with suitably spartan furnishings. A man sat propped up in the narrow bed. At the sight of his wan face, Margarita exclaimed involuntarily, "Father Vicente!"

The priest lifted a thin hand and peered at them through the gloom. "Margarita? Margarita Salazar?"

"Sí, Father," she said, coming forward. "What has happened to you?" They had been told that the priest was wounded, but seeing him like this had obviously shaken her.

"Peace, child. I am fine, just a bit weak right now."

From the doorway, the man who had brought them back here said, "Guerrero shot him. The dog—"

"Please, Pablo," Father Vicente said. "I have told you, your anger will only hurt yourself. Guerrero cannot feel it in his home in the mountains."

Buffalo stepped up next to Margarita. "Reckon that's why we're here, padre," he said. "We're lookin' for this feller Guerrero's hideout."

The priest's eyes widened a bit as he took in Buffalo's massive shape. "And who are you, my son?"

"Name's Buffalo Newcomb." he grinned. "And no offense, padre, but I ain't your son. My daddy was part mountain lion, part grizzly bear, part snappin' turtle, and all liar."

"Ah," Father Vicente said. "Then you are a Texan."

Daniels swallowed the laugh that tried to come up his throat. He said, "So am I, padre. My name is Curtis Daniels, and like Buffalo says, we're looking for Ignacio Guerrero."

Rafael stepped forward. "I am Rafael Sebastiano y Roderigo Vasquez," he said. "There were two women with Guerrero when he was here?"

Father Vicente nodded. "Yes, two young women, both very beautiful."

"And were they all right?"

"I . . . do not know, Señor Vasquez. They appeared to be so."

Rafael breathed a prayer of thanksgiving. "One of them is my cousin Angelina," he explained. "Guerrero and his men killed her parents."

"I can believe that, my son," Father Vicente said solemnly. His eyes moved to Margarita again. "And what is that you have there?"

"My daughter, Antonia," she said quietly, shy now. Moving closer to the bed, she pulled back the blankets to reveal the face of the sleeping infant.

"Ah . . ." Father Vicente raised his hand and touched the downy hair on top of the baby's head. "Such a beautiful child." His glance flicked to Margarita. "And your husband? Where is he?"

Margarita bit her lower lip and was unable to answer.

After a moment, Daniels said, "Apaches killed him, Father. We buried him out on his place as proper as we could. Of course, it wasn't the same as if we'd been able to bring him here, so that you could have done things right, but . . ."

"I understand, Señor Daniels. And I assure you, you did the correct thing." He took a deep breath. "Margarita, you and your child are welcome to stay here with us. I am sure Pablo can find a place . . ."

"Sí," Pablo said. "Come with me, señora. I will take you to the women."

Margarita looked at Daniels, and he nodded. "You go ahead. It's for the best. We'll see you later. Reckon we'd better talk to the padre a little more first, though."

"Do not tire him," Pablo warned darkly as he took Margarita's arm and gently steered her toward the door of the chamber.

Father Vicente laughed softly. "You are like the hens with their chicks, Pablo. These gentlemen and I will speak together, and then I will rest."

"See that you do, Father," Pablo said as he went out with Margarita and Antonia.

Buffalo drew up a chair, reversed it, and straddled it. The leather thongs that bound it together creaked under the strain, but they held. "So," the big man said, "Guerrero shot you. He have a reason, or'd he do it just out o' sheer cussedness?"

"I refused to bow down before him," Father Vicente replied, a hint of the anger he felt at the memory in his voice.

"Why'd he want you to do that?"

"Because he intends to rule this land, señor. According to a kitchen servant who witnessed the incident, Guerrero told one of the women with him that he is going to be the king of the Sierra Madre."

Buffalo snorted. "King of the Sierra Madre," he repeated. "Mighty highfalutin title for a low-down bandit like Guerrero. You reckon he can do it?"

"Who knows what is possible?" the priest answered

with a shrug. "I think it unlikely. But Guerrero could shed much innocent blood in the attempt—unless someone stops him."

Rafael leaned forward. "You said something about Guerrero's home in the mountains. Do you know where it is?"

Father Vicente shook his head. "Since he came and brought his evil to our home, I have heard much about him from the people. It is known that at one time, he occupied a stronghold in the Sierra Madre, a house of stone that not even an army could conquer. But he left it to ride the plains, to rob and kill and gather other evil men to ride with him."

Daniels felt a twinge of guilt as he listened to those words. He had been one of those "other evil men" who had joined Guerrero's band. But the priest didn't know that.

"Now he is going back," Father Vicente went on. "He intends to marry one of the women who were with him. It seems she is wealthy, and Guerrero thinks that he will get his hands on her money. At least this is what the servant in the kitchen overheard."

Buffalo glanced over his shoulder at Daniels and Rafael. "Doña Isabella," he grunted. "Reckon Guerrero really is mad. Her folks and Don Hortensio's family might hand over a wad of ransom money to get her back, but they ain't goin' to pay a thing if he up an' marries her! They'd as soon see her dead, once that happens."

Father Vicente looked at Rafael. "You say Guerrero has your cousin?"

"*Sí*. She is the other woman, the one he does not plan to marry."

The priest's eyes moved to Buffalo and Daniels. "I understand why your companion pursues Guerrero. What about the two of you?"

"Reckon you could say it's personal with us, too, padre," Buffalo said. "You see, when Guerrero raided that cantina where he grabbed them gals, he rode off and left Daniels an' me for dead. You can still see some of the blood that was spilled when we fought off them *bandidos*. So we got a grudge to settle, too."

Rafael frowned but said nothing. Daniels had tensed up when the priest asked the question, but Buffalo's answer had come as a surprise. The big man must have had a reason for concealing Daniels's connection with Guerrero's gang. Daniels couldn't understand it, but he was grateful for the lie that Buffalo told.

Father Vicente sighed. "As I told Pablo, vengeance serves no purpose. However, to protect the innocent and to rescue those poor unfortunate young señoritas, someone must find Guerrero and deal with him. If that is your mission, señores, I will pray that you have much good fortune and remain safe."

"We ain't goin' to stay safe, not and find Guerrero," Buffalo said, "but if you're in a prayin' mood, we'd settle for stayin' alive, wouldn't we, boys?"

"And getting those girls out alive," Daniels added.

Father Vicente lowered his head. "So shall I pray."

Buffalo stood up. "We'll let you get your rest, padre. Reckon it'll be all right for us to stay here tonight?"

"Of course. I will have a meal prepared for you, and Pablo will show you where you can sleep. Your animals will be cared for, as well."

"Thanks, padre. We'll be leavin' early in the mornin'." Buffalo grinned. "We got us a king to find, and when we do—sorry, padre—we're goin' to kick his ass right off his throne."

ELEVEN

IT WAS AMAZING WHAT a difference a hot meal and a few cups of wine could make in the way a man felt. Life almost seemed worth living again, Curtis Daniels thought as he leaned against an adobe pillar and looked up at the night sky.

He was standing on the covered walkway in front of some storerooms that made up one wing of the mission. To his right were the foothills, rising sharply from the plains and lifting to the majestic range of mountains. To Daniels's left was the semidesert he and his companions had just crossed. That journey had worn him down more than he had realized. Danger, heat, and guilt had drained him to the point that the only thing keeping him going had been his tightly stretched nerves.

That had changed now. The comfortably full feeling in his belly, the cool, gentle wind from the mountains, the pinpricks of light against the looming darkness that marked the positions of the stars in the heavens . . . Those things had calmed him, brought peace to his heart for the first time in months.

The feeling wouldn't last. He knew that. Come morning, he and Buffalo and Rafael would be leaving this haven and starting after Guerrero again. There would be more blood and death before any of them could rest like this again—if indeed that chance ever came.

But for the moment, by God, he was going to enjoy the tranquility.

"If'n I was Guerrero, you'd be dead right about now, son," a gravelly voice rumbled from behind him.

Recognizing Buffalo Newcomb's distinctive tones, Daniels turned around slowly and saw the starlight shining on the big man's teeth revealed in his habitual grin. It didn't seem possible that anyone as large as Buffalo could come up on him that quietly, but that was what had happened.

"I didn't hear you," Daniels said.

Buffalo scratched a lucifer into life and held the flame to a short cigar that looked like a piece of black rope. "Reckon that's mighty clear," he grunted as he got the cigar going. "Don't know if I want to chase outlaws with you or not, boy, if you're goin' to stand around with your head all muddied up like that."

Daniels grimaced in the shadows. He had let the Apaches sneak up on them back at the Salazar jacal, too, and he was waiting for Buffalo to bring that up. Some people just weren't cut out to be adventurers, he supposed. Oh, he could use a gun all right and he was good with his fists, but he seemed to lack that knack for survival that distinguished longtime frontiersmen like Buffalo Newcomb.

Where he really ought to be, Daniels suddenly realized, was back on a farm somewhere, working the land instead of chasing *bandidos* through the mountains of Mexico.

"Sorry," he said when Buffalo didn't continue. "I guess I got to feeling too safe. It's not likely Guerrero's going to come back here, not after hitting the place so recently."

"Reckon that's true. And the Injuns generally leave these missions alone these days. But that ain't no excuse for not havin' your eyes open."

Daniels felt a sudden surge of resentment at Buffalo's chiding tone. "Don't you ever relax?" he demanded.

"Don't you ever stop worrying about killing somebody or else they'll kill you?"

Buffalo sent a cloud of smoke into the air as he exhaled. "You just answered your own question, boy," he said as he pointed the glowing tip of the cigar at Daniels.

Daniels shook his head and bit back his anger. To change the subject, he asked, "Where's Rafael?"

"Talkin' to that feller Pablo, last time I saw. He's tryin' to find out as much about Guerrero as he can. Good idea. Always pays to know your enemy."

"You plan on pulling out first thing in the morning?"

Buffalo nodded his shaggy head. "No point in waitin' around here. There's hundreds of hidey-holes up in them mountains, an' the sooner we start lookin', the sooner we'll find Guerrero." He gave Daniels a shrewd look, put the cigar back in his mouth, and spoke around it. "Reckon you've decided you'd rather stay here."

"What makes you think that?"

"The padre an' his flock'd be glad to take you in, even if you are a gringo. And you'd have you a ready-made family."

Daniels gave him a puzzled glance but couldn't read Buffalo's expression in the gloom. "What does that mean?"

"That gal Margarita and her baby . . . They'd be right happy to have you around. Gal needs a husband, baby needs a daddy."

Daniels couldn't keep the surprise and anger out of his voice. "Dammit, Buffalo, she's only been a widow for a few days. Her husband's barely cold in the ground, for God's sake! And you're talking about me marrying her?"

"I've seen the way she looks at you, heard the way she sounds when she talks to you. She wouldn't mind a bit, son. You can take my word for it."

Daniels snorted and said, "Seems like there's a lot of things I'm supposed to take your word for."

"Generally speakin', that's a mighty fine idea." The tip of the cigar glowed bright red as Buffalo inhaled.

"Well, you can forget about this one," Daniels replied emphatically. "I'm going after Guerrero with you and Rafael. Like the priest said, somebody's got to stop Guerrero."

"Could always come back here when we're done," Buffalo suggested.

"If we're still alive, you mean."

The big man inclined his head in acknowledgment. "There is that." Buffalo sighed. "Reckon a man could do worse. This place is mighty peaceful."

"Maybe you're the one who'd like to stay," Daniels said mockingly. "You could become a priest like Father Vicente, take vows of chastity and poverty."

Buffalo threw back his head and laughed. "Ain't never had no trouble bein' poor, but that chastity business could get a mite difficult. 'Sides, boy, can you imagine me in one o' them robes?"

Daniels had to shake his head and smile. The image summoned up by Buffalo's question was a ludicrous one, all right.

"Maybe once we're through with Guerrero, we should both head for someplace different," he said. "There's plenty of places I haven't been."

"Well, that ain't the case with me, since I done been ever'where and seen ever' elephant there is to see. Reckon there's some I wouldn't mind seein' again, though." Buffalo drew deeply on the cigar one more time, then dropped the butt and snuffed it out with his boot. "Best get some sleep, son. We'll be ridin' early."

He turned and lumbered away.

Daniels watched him go and thought again about the twists of fate that had brought him here. He could just as easily have been lying dead in that ditch behind the Vasquez cantina.

But he wasn't. He was alive, and he suddenly realized that he was going to hang on to that and savor it for as long as he could.

• • •

Daniels pulled the cinch tight and stepped back to survey the job he had done of saddling the mule. Everything looked in order.

They had saddled by lanternlight. The sky was still black and flecked with stars overhead, although grayness was beginning to creep in from the eastern horizon. Buffalo had meant it when he said they would be leaving early.

Daniels had been groggy when the big man shook him awake in the little bedchamber he had been given for the night. A couple of cups of strong black coffee had opened his eyes and cleared away some of the cobwebs from his brain. There were plenty of tortillas and bacon and eggs for breakfast, and Daniels had eaten his fill. Pablo's claim that Guerrero's men had stolen all of the mission's provisions had been an exaggeration. The *bandidos* had gotten the extra stores, but with plenty of cattle and pigs and goats and chickens, in addition to the carefully cultivated fields, the people of San Cristóbal would never go hungry. In addition, the packs on the backs of the extra mules and the saddlebags slung on the mounts were now filled with supplies. Buffalo estimated they had enough food for a couple of weeks if they were careful.

Father Vicente limped from the church into the plaza, his leg wrapped with bulky bandages under the cassock he wore. Pablo was at the priest's side, as usual, supporting Father Vicente with a hand under his arm. Several men and women trailed them out of the church.

"We will pray for you," Father Vicente said as Daniels, Buffalo, and Rafael swung up and settled into their saddles. "*Vaya con Dios*, my friends."

"Thanks, padre," Buffalo said. "Reckon we can use all the help we can get."

Margarita Salazar emerged from the small knot of people behind the priest and hurried forward to reach up and grasp Daniels's hand. Surprised by her action, he sat there not knowing what to do, leaving his hand where it was and feeling the warmth of her fingers.

"Please be careful, Senor Daniels," she said with a catch in her voice. "Antonia and I . . . we owe you so much."

"No, ma'am," he said. "You don't owe me a thing. You just take good care of yourself and that baby."

Father Vicente spoke again, his voice stronger this morning despite the pallor that still showed on his face. "If you ride this way again, gentlemen, please stop. San Cristóbal would be honored by your presence."

Buffalo tugged his hat down. "We'll do that, padre." He wheeled his horse. "Let's go."

Rafael lifted a hand and called, "*Adiós*," to several of the people watching their departure, then turned to follow Buffalo. Daniels hesitated, then slid his hand out of Margarita's grasp and pulled on the reins of his mule. The animal swung around and started following the others as Daniels dug his heels into its sides. He led one of the pack mules, Buffalo and Rafael taking the other two.

It was probably a mistake to look back, Daniels thought, but he did it anyway as he rode away. Margarita still stood apart from the others and a little in front, her hand lifted in a gesture of farewell. He returned the wave, then sternly told himself to turn his attention forward. Looking back wasn't going to help anybody.

Sleep had not come easily for him the night before, which had only added to his grogginess come morning. He had found himself staring up at the bare ceiling of the little room and thinking about what Buffalo had said. The big man was probably right; Margarita would have welcomed that sort of interest from him, even newly widowed as she was. Although she had claimed to care very much for her late husband, she had made a point of saying that she had not loved him at the time of their marriage. And she had never said that she came to love him later, either.

She was pretty enough, Daniels supposed. A little skinny, but time and plenty of decent food would take care of that. And she was young, of course, but not that much younger than Willa had been when he married her.

Margarita's husband was dead, and so was his wife. There was no reason in the world why the two of them shouldn't get together.

Except for the fact that Daniels had never felt anything for her except pity at first, then admiration at her surprising strength. Those things might be important, but they didn't add up to love.

Besides, he had been drifting for quite a while now. As peaceful and appealing as life at San Cristóbal might seem on the surface, he knew he couldn't be happy at the mission. Being fiddle-footed was too deeply ingrained in him by now.

If he survived this search for Guerrero, Daniels suddenly decided as he rode away from the mission with Buffalo and Rafael, he wouldn't be coming back to San Cristóbal. Margarita would probably think he was dead, and he hated the idea of causing her that pain, but eventually she would forget him. And that would be better all around.

Of course, if they met up with Guerrero, he probably would wind up dead. Then he wouldn't have to worry about any of this.

He had caught up to Buffalo and Rafael and was riding between them. Buffalo glanced over at him in the gray light and said, "You're lookin' mighty grim, boy."

"I was just thinking . . ." Daniels began, then realized that he couldn't share those thoughts with his two companions. He went on, "I was wondering what we're going to do when—and if—we find Guerrero's stronghold."

"Sí," Rafael added. "I have pondered this question myself, Senor Buffalo."

"Well, first off, there ain't no if about it. We'll find the place. May take a while, but I know those mountains pretty well. Guerrero can't hope to hide out forever in 'em. When we do cut his trail again, we'll foller it 'til we got him located. Then, once we got the lay o' the land, we'll figger out the best way to get in, grab them gals, and get back out."

Daniels nodded. He said, "Guerrero doesn't know about Rafael, and he thinks you and I are dead. Maybe he won't be expecting any trouble."

"Won't matter a whole hell of a lot whether he knows about us. If he's tryin' to raise an army to take over this part of the country, he's goin' to have his eyes open. Ain't goin' to be easy to sneak up on him. Reckon we'll have to figger out a way, though."

"I have studied the world's greatest military minds," Rafael said proudly. "I am sure that I will be able to formulate a successful strategy based on the tactics of Caesar, Alexander, and Napoleon."

"I've heard tell of that French feller, since it's his nephew who helped make ol' Maximilian emperor over here, but the other two I ain't heard of. They Texans or Yankees?"

"Caesar was the Emperor of Rome," Rafael said stiffly. "Alexander the Great was the most powerful general the world has ever seen. He conquered most of the civilized world during his time."

"And I'll bet neither one o' those fellers ever fought bandits in the Sierra Madre, did they? Well, did they?" Buffalo insisted when Rafael didn't answer.

"Of course not," the Mexican finally said. "They lived hundreds of years ago."

"Then they don't know sic 'em about chasin' down *bandidos*." Buffalo jabbed himself in the chest with a blunt thumb. "I do. I've done the chasin', and I been chased a time or two myself. So you just pay attention to me, boy, and maybe you'll come through this alive."

Daniels had listened to the exchange with interest, trying not to grin. Rafael muttered something under his breath, then said grudgingly, "*Sí*. I will pay attention to you, Señor Buffalo."

The three of them rode on toward the mountains as the sun rose behind them.

They were never going to see level ground again. Daniels was certain of that.

For nearly two weeks—Daniels was unsure of exactly

how much time had passed since they had left San Cristóbal—they had been riding up and down the forested slopes of the Sierra Madre. The going was rough, and mules and men were all exhausted. Daniels slept on hard, rocky ground at night and hung on to a swaying, bouncing saddle all day.

They had seen few people since entering the mountains and had spoken to no one. Buffalo had spotted a few widely scattered ranchos and farms, but he always steered them around the places. "Word gets around faster'n you'd think up here," he explained. "We go to stoppin' and askin' about Guerrero at ever' place we come to, he's goin' to hear about it."

"Then how will we find him?" Rafael asked in exasperation. "Do you expect to just stumble over him?"

"Daniels here said the hideout was supposed to be near a valley where there was a village," Buffalo pointed out. "I been lookin' for that valley. Once we find it, we'll find Guerrero's stronghold, I reckon."

"I thought you knew all of the . . . how did you put it, 'hidey-holes' in these mountains. Are you saying that you are lost, Senor Buffalo?" Rafael's voice was arch and dripping with scorn.

That was a dangerous attitude to take, Daniels thought as he glanced at Buffalo's darkly scowling features.

Buffalo reached down to scratch Stink's ears as they rode along. The possum reacted angrily, as usual, writhing in the bag in an attempt to get at the hand that was touching him. Buffalo reached back, caught the tail that was protruding from the opening at the other end of the bag, and lifted it. The tail lashed around for a second, then wrapped itself around his thick wrist. "Settle down, varmint," Buffalo warned. "You get too feisty, I'm liable to chop me off a possum tail." He looked up at Rafael. "We'll find the place. Just don't you get feisty on me, neither."

"We shall wait and see," Rafael shot back.

"Damn right we will."

Daniels wanted to tell both of them to shut up. Where

they got the energy to argue, he didn't know. It was taking all of his strength just to put in the long hours in the saddle every day.

That evening, as Daniels dug through their packs and prepared another cold supper, he said, "We're going to be running out of supplies in another day or two. We'd better start keeping an eye out for deer. . . . Unless you want to try to buy some provisions at one of those ranches, Buffalo."

"There's plenty of game hereabouts," Buffalo said with a shake of his head. "No need to go announcin' we're here by ridin' in to some rancho."

"If Guerrero is bent on terrorizing the inhabitants of this area, why do you insist there is a danger of them helping him by carrying word of our search?" Rafael wanted to know. He sat with his back against a small boulder, legs stretched out in front of him, ankles crossed, sombrero lying at his side.

"There's a simple little reason for that: fear. Reckon the first thing Guerrero did when he rode back into the mountains was spread the word to folks that he was back and takin' over, that anybody who didn't cooperate'd be killed."

Daniels said, "He left that cantina with five men. That's not enough to back up a threat like that."

"We don't know how many riders he's picked up since then," Buffalo pointed out. "And sometimes it don't matter how many men you really got on your side, long as you can convince folks that they're outnumbered. I figger a gent like Guerrero's probably pretty good at that."

Buffalo was right, Daniels thought. Fear was a large part of Guerrero's power. He was Ignacio Guerrero, the legendary bandit, and he made sure that everyone knew it. He was probably running a bluff just like a veteran poker player.

On the other hand, it was always possible that Guerrero had been able to recruit quite a few men in the time that they had been searching for him. When they finally did find the stronghold, it might easily hold several dozen *bandidos*, all of them nearly as ruthless as Guerrero himself.

A small shudder ran through Daniels as he imagined Angelina Vasquez and Isabella Alvarez trapped in that situation.

It wouldn't do any good to dwell on those thoughts. Daniels tried to take his mind off them by passing out the tortillas and beans and jerky. He remembered the dinner at San Cristóbal—the succulent slices of ham, the pan bread and wild honey, the crisp ears of corn. . . .

Buffalo Newcomb leaned over, accepted a tortilla from Daniels, and cut through the young Texan's memories by saying, "Don't take no note of it right off, but there's folks out there in the brush watchin' us, and they got guns."

TWELVE

DANIELS STIFFENED AND SAID, "What?"

Buffalo's voice was uncommonly quiet, maybe the quietest Daniels had ever heard it. "I said there's fellers out there watchin' us, and they're heeled."

Daniels glanced over at Rafael. The Mexican was busy eating and appeared not to have heard the warning. That was good, Daniels thought. As long as Rafael was so unconcerned, the watchers might believe they had been unnoticed.

"How many?"

"Don't know for sure, but there's too many for us to jump 'em," Buffalo said. "And they're all around us, which don't help matters none. You just sit tight, Curtis. Ain't nothin' we can do now but wait and see what they want."

Daniels grimaced. "But what if they're planning to ambush us?"

"They'd've done it 'fore now, happen that was what they had in mind."

Around a mouthful of tortilla, Rafael asked, "What are you two muttering about? You sound like two old hens clucking to each other."

"Maybe we're tryin' to hatch up some trouble," Buffalo replied with a grin.

Rafael frowned at him. "You are making the joke, no?"

"Nope, no joke—"

Buffalo broke off his reply as a crackling came from the brush that surrounded the small mountainside clearing. The noise was clearly audible to Daniels and Rafael as well. Rafael sat up sharply, reaching for the rifle that lay next to him. Buffalo snapped, "Hold it, boy! Leave that alone."

Figures stepped out of the brush, vague shapes in the moonlight at first that slowly resolved themselves into men holding guns. Daniels turned his head and counted eight of them; not that many, really, but the way they were spread out, they had him and Buffalo and Rafael surrounded. If any shooting started, the three of them would be caught in a deadly cross fire.

"*Hola, amigos,*" one of the strangers said cheerfully. "What are you doing, sitting here in the cold and dark on the side of a mountain?"

"Happens we like it, mister," Buffalo answered. "What business is it of yours?"

"Oh, a gringo . . . Well, señor, it is our business because we own this mountain, and you and your friends are trespassing."

Rafael snorted in disbelief. "No one owns a mountain," he declared.

"That is where you are wrong," the man told him. "We do own it. Or rather, our master does."

Daniels was staring around at their captors. The men wore jackets against the chill in the mountain air, but otherwise they were dressed much as he was. All of them carried rifles, and each man wore a six-gun, as well. Several had bandoliers of ammunition crisscrossed across their torsos. A few of them also carried machetes in fringed leather scabbards.

There was no doubt in Daniels's mind who their "leader" was. These had to be some of Guerrero's men. Even as that thought came to him, he realized that one of the bandits was staring at him, trying to make out his features in the silvery illumination of the newly risen moon. Daniels dropped his head and gritted his teeth against the curse that sprang to his lips. The man's name was Zacateca, or some such, and he had been one of the men who had ridden with Guerrero at the same time Daniels had been part of the gang.

"Look, feller," Buffalo said. "We don't mean no harm by bein' here. We're just passin' through. So why don't you let us go on our way, and we'll be off your boss's mountain first thing in the mornin'."

The Mexican who had spoken before shook his head. "I cannot do that, señor. We have our orders. Anyone caught trespassing on our master's property must be brought before him for his personal attention. We will camp here tonight, and then in the morning we will take you to see him." The man waved a hand toward the north. "It is not far. Half a day's ride, perhaps."

Rafael started to protest, but Buffalo silenced him with a curt gesture. The big man turned back to the bandit and asked, "What you reckon this master of yours is goin' to do with us?"

The Mexican shrugged. "Perhaps nothing, if you show him the proper respect and if you have sufficient valuables in your belongings." Again the shrug. "If not, well, then I am sorry, señores. We will have the unpleasant task of shooting you."

"I was afraid you was goin' to say that," Buffalo sighed.

The leader rapped an order, and two men stepped forward to hastily pick up the prisoners' rifles and jerk the Colt from Rafael's holster. "Light a fire," the spokesman told another man. "There is no need for us to sit shivering in the dark."

There was plenty of wood and brush around. In just a few minutes, a small blaze was leaping and dancing in the center of the clearing. Buffalo, Daniels, and Rafael remained where they were. The attitude of the bandits eased somewhat now that the three prisoners had been disarmed.

Daniels kept his head down, not wanting Zacateca to recognize him. Of course, if they were taken before Guerrero, the discovery of his true identity was a foregone conclusion. The self-styled king of the Sierra Madre would probably recognize Buffalo, too. And most certain of all was the fact that Guerrero would immediately order them killed.

Buffalo had to know that. What the hell was he waiting for? Better to go down fighting now, Daniels thought, than wait to be executed by Guerrero.

One of the bandits was sent back for their horses, which had been tied in the trees a considerable distance away. Once the horses had been brought up to the camp, another man fetched a pan from his pack and began to cook some coffee. The leader sank down cross-legged across the flames from Buffalo. He appeared to be completely at ease now. Two men were standing near the prisoners, rifles trained on them at all times.

"How'd you spot us?" Buffalo asked. "Not that we was hidin', mind you, but I've learned it don't pay to call much attention to yourself around these parts."

"That is very wise," the Mexican agreed. "However, a vaquero noticed you just before dusk and brought word to us. The people who live in these mountains know that it is prudent to keep us advised of any comings and goings."

Just like Buffalo had said, Daniels thought. Guerrero already had the common folks so scared that they would do anything he said. Maybe Guerrero's dream of taking over this part of the country wasn't so farfetched after all.

Buffalo nodded toward the fire. "Mind sharin' some of that coffee when it's ready?"

"Of course not. It is the least we can do, señor."

Since you know you're going to be blowing our heads off tomorrow, Daniels thought bleakly. He glanced around. Two men were tending to the horses, two were standing guard over the prisoners, and two had drifted off into the forest, no doubt to serve as sentries. That left the leader and the man making the coffee.

Bad odds, all the way around. But likely the best ones they were going to get.

His eyes flicked to the rifles that had been taken away from them. They were stacked on the other side of the fire, too far away to reach quickly. He and Buffalo and Rafael still had their knives, but those weren't much good against rifles.

"That's one of them machetes, ain't it?" Buffalo asked suddenly, pointing at the scabbard on the leader's hip. "I've always wanted to have one of them things."

"Yes, they are fine blades," the Mexican said, sliding the oversized knife out of its sheath. "I would let you take a closer look at it, but under the circumstances . . . you understand."

"Sure," Buffalo agreed.

The Mexican wrinkled his nose, looking around, his face twisting in displeasure. "What is that smell?"

Stink picked that moment to come waddling out of the darkness, making his way slowly toward the warmth of the fire.

The hand of the bandit leader tightened on the machete's hilt as he spotted the ungainly looking animal. *"Dios!"* he exclaimed angrily. "What sort of vermin is that?"

He slashed at the possum with the machete, the broad blade winking in the firelight.

Buffalo Newcomb threw himself across the flames with a roar, scattering the blazing brands and slamming into the Mexican. Buffalo's fingers caught the man's wrist before the machete could strike Stink. The Mexican screamed as bones splintered.

Instinctively, Daniels flung himself to the side. An instant later, a rifle blasted, sending a bullet through the spot where he had been. He landed rolling and kicked up, his boot impacting the barrel of the second guard's rifle and knocking it aside even as the man fired at Buffalo. Daniels grabbed the bandit's legs and jerked them out from under him.

Buffalo's left fist crashed into the leader's jaw while his right hand ground the broken bones together in the man's wrist. The Mexican dropped the machete and sprawled limply underneath the big man. Buffalo let go of him, snatched up the fallen machete, and rolled to the side as more of the bandits came running to join the fight.

Daniels got one hand on the guard's rifle and the other on the man's throat. He wrenched the weapon free and jabbed it at his opponent, driving the butt into the center of the man's face. He felt the guard go limp.

What the hell was Rafael doing? Daniels wondered as he twisted around to look for another enemy.

He spotted Rafael on the ground a few yards away, grappling with the other guard. Beyond them, men were pouring into the circle of light cast by the camp fire, which had blazed up again after Buffalo had crashed over it.

Buffalo was still on the ground when one of the bandits loomed over him, almost running past him before being able to stop. The man tried to bring his rifle to bear, but he was too late.

Buffalo slashed straight up between the bandit's legs with the machete.

Daniels saw the spurt of blood and heard the screech, but then he was too busy to devote any more attention to the gruesome sight. A bullet whined past his head as he dove toward one of the fallen rifles. It was an old Colt Carbine with a six-shot cylinder, but Daniels had no way of knowing how many of the chambers were loaded. All he could do was grab it up, point it at the bandits surging toward him, and start cocking and firing.

The rifle bucked in his hands, the roar of the shots deafening as it echoed back from the side of the mountain. He thought he heard the sharper cracks of a handgun, but he wasn't sure. It was hard to see anything through the haze of powder smoke that drifted in front of his eyes. The hammer of the carbine fell on an exploded chamber. Daniels came to his feet, reversing the rifle and gripping the hot barrel. With a shrill cry, he threw himself forward, ready to use the carbine as a club.

A strong arm caught him around the middle and held him back. Buffalo shouted, "Hold it! Hold on there! Dammit, they're all dead! Now settle down, Curtis!"

Panting, sweat running into his eyes despite the coldness of the night, Daniels stood there, his hands still clutching the uplifted rifle. Finally, he looked around, saw Buffalo's blood-streaked face, and forced himself to take a deep breath.

"Dead?" he asked. "All dead?"

"Sí," Rafael answered from nearby, a fierce exultation in his voice unlike anything Daniels had heard there before. Daniels looked around and saw a Colt in the Mexican's hand. Obviously, Rafael had grabbed it from one of the fallen bandits and put it to good use.

Buffalo released Daniels and stepped back. In his other hand, he held the machete, its blade no longer shiny but dull now with a thick coating of blood. Daniels looked past Buffalo at a scene of carnage and suddenly felt sick. There was blood splashed everywhere, and dead men who didn't seem to be all in one piece. . . .

Buffalo grabbed his arm as he started to double over and retch. "Ain't time for that," the big man said. "We got to gather up all the guns we can get our hands on and get out of here. Somebody else might've heard those shots and got curious. We don't want to be around here when them bodies're found."

Daniels forced back the bile in his throat and nodded weakly. Damn right he didn't want to stay around here. What he had seen already would haunt him for a long time, he thought.

As if reading his mind, Buffalo tightened his grasp on Daniels's arm and said, "Nope, it ain't pretty. But it beats bein' dead, and that's what we'd've been if we'd let them boys take us to Guerrero's hideout as prisoners. Now come on, blast it."

Daniels went.

• • •

Dawn found them on a rocky bench high on the side of a mountain, north of the spot where they had fought with Guerrero's men. Buffalo had kept them moving until they had covered a couple of miles from the site of the massacre, then let them stop to rest for the remainder of the night. "No point in riskin' gettin' lost or fallin' in a hole," he had said. "We're far enough away now. Come mornin', we'll head north again and see if we can find that hideout Guerrero's man said was this way."

That sounded like a good plan to Daniels. He was glad for the opportunity to stop and rest, but on the other hand, once they had come to a halt, he didn't have as much to occupy his mind. As long as he had been concentrating on staying on the back of the mule as it negotiated the steep slopes, he didn't have time to think about all the killing he had just been a part of.

Now he could remember the blood and the hacked-apart bodies. . . .

He didn't get much sleep, and that wasn't totally due to the cold, hard ground. By the time the sky lightened with approaching day, he was more than ready to get up. With any luck, they would reach Guerrero's stronghold today. Their quest was almost over.

Buffalo didn't waste any time in getting them moving again. Before the sun had completely cleared the horizon, the three men were riding north once more, carefully descending the peak they were on and starting up the next one. Daniels's muscles creaked painfully. If they ever got back to civilization, he vowed, he was going to find a barbershop that offered baths, sink down in as hot a tub as he could stand, and not move for a week.

Guerrero's henchman had claimed the stronghold was half a day's ride north. By noon, Daniels hadn't seen any sign of the valley that was supposed to be nearby. When he said as much, Buffalo replied, "Could be we're a mite off. Could be the feller was wrong. Let's keep ridin' and lookin'. We'll run across the place."

Daniels wished he could share that optimism. They had been searching for so long now; he was starting to believe they would never find Guerrero's hideout.

They were eating tortillas and jerky in the saddle a little later when Buffalo reined in, pointed, and said, "Look there."

Daniels's gaze followed the big man's blunt finger, and he stiffened as he saw a thin line of smoke against the sky. "You think that's it?" he asked.

"It must be," Rafael said excitedly before Buffalo could answer. "Who else but a madman would be out here in the middle of this godforsaken wilderness?"

"*We're* out here," Buffalo said. "But I reckon you're right. That smoke's prob'ly comin' from either Guerrero's place or that village close by. Either way, we're on the right trail. Come on." He spurred his mule ahead, Daniels and Rafael following close behind him.

They had to come down off the mountain, skirt another height, and then twist along a narrow path that led them through a gully before they reached a spot that would give them a view of the smoke's origin. That took them a little over an hour. But at the end of that time, they were able to look down into a long, narrow valley that was closed off by cliffs on the far end, making it look something like a box canyon. There was a setback about halfway up the cliffs, forming another bench, and that was where a huge stone structure sat. It was hard to be sure at this distance, but it seemed to be built along the lines of a typical hacienda, except for the fact that it was constructed of stone rather than adobe. Given the size of the place, there was probably a large courtyard in the center of it. A wide path leading up to the bench had been hacked into the rock of the cliff. It was an imposing sight.

"A fittin' palace for a king," Buffalo muttered as he stared across the valley. "But not for a skunk like Guerrero."

"That must be the place," Rafael said. "It fits the description."

"Sure, that's it," Buffalo agreed. "Now, how do we get into it?"

Daniels said, "We can't ride through the valley and up that path. They'd see us coming a mile off."

Buffalo was frowning as he studied the terrain. "Them cliffs behind the house look sheer, but I'm bettin' they ain't. Guerrero may be as lowdown as they come, but he ain't stupid. There's got to be a back door out o' there."

"*Sí,*" Rafael nodded. "That path leading up would be easily defended, but in turn it would be simple to prevent Guerrero from leaving that way. Without another route to and from the house, he would be, how do you say, bottled up."

"So that's what we're going to have to find," Daniels said. "That back door is our way in."

Buffalo nodded. "Maybe. But Guerrero may have it guarded, too." He clucked to his mule and lifted the reins. "Come on. First thing we got to do is get around this valley."

As Buffalo led them back toward the high country, Daniels glanced down again at the valley they were going to bypass. A stream trickled through the center of it, probably emerging from the cliffs at the far end, under the house. That provided enough water for the fields. It was unusual to find enough tillable soil in these mountains to make farming possible, but from the looks of it, these fields were fertile. He would see corn and wheat and beans growing. There was a cluster of huts about midway up the valley where the peasants who worked the fields would live. Like the area around San Cristóbal, this was a surprisingly pretty place in the middle of a generally ugly land.

But the massive stone house looming over the valley made it seem as if clouds overhung the fields and the huts, even though the sun was shining. It squatted there like some kind of obscene toad. That impression was only because he knew who was occupying it now, Daniels thought. As Buffalo had said, the place would make a good palace for a real king—instead of a bloodthirsty bandit.

It was time to depose Guerrero and return peace to this valley. Those were mighty high-flown sentiments, Daniels told himself, but true nonetheless.

He just wished his heart would stop pounding so hard and his throat would quit being so dry that he couldn't swallow.

T·H·I·R·T·E·E·N

"WE'LL START DOWN SOON as it gets good an' dark,"
Buffalo said as he crouched behind a boulder at the edge
of the cliff. "If we can get down on that bench 'fore the
moon comes up, I reckon there's a good chance they
won't spot us."

Daniels knelt nearby, like Buffalo and Rafael staying
far enough back from the rim that they wouldn't be
seen from the house below. He remembered the queasy
feeling he had experienced when he crawled up to the
edge of the cliff with the others and peered over at the
narrow steps cut into the rock. They were little more
than hand- and footholds, and now Buffalo was proposing that they climb down in the dark.

On the other hand, if they tried it while it was still
light and were seen, Guerrero's men could pick them off
easily, just like swatting flies on a wall.

"Rafe, you'll stay here," Buffalo went on.

"What?" Rafael exclaimed. "I am no coward to be
left behind, señor—"

"Never said you was," Buffalo cut in. "But somebody's got to stay up here with the mules. 'Sides, if
there's trouble, you can cover us from the rim. Curtis
an' me'll find them gals and bring 'em out."

That made sense to Daniels. They were well armed

now with the weapons they had taken from the bodies of Guerrero's men. It would be hard to carry rifles down the face of the cliff, so he and Buffalo could leave theirs with Rafael, giving him plenty of firepower. And if there was any pursuit from the house, the Mexican would be in a perfect position to provide them with covering fire.

It had taken most of the afternoon to work their way around the valley and into this position above the cliffs. The path leading here was steep, but the mules had been able to negotiate it. Daniels wouldn't have wanted to try it in a hurry, though; he and the others had allowed their mounts to pick their own way, at their own pace.

Once they had reached this spot, they had been able to get a better look at Guerrero's stronghold. In addition to the big stone house, the bench some fifty feet below them contained two stands of trees, one on each side of the building. There were several other smaller buildings as well, stone huts that had probably been intended as quarters for the vaqueros of the rancher who must have built this place. Now the outbuildings no doubt housed Guerrero's men, and some of them were probably used for storage, too. There was a barn and a good-sized corral at the base of the lower cliff, where the bandits' horses were kept.

Daniels had seen a few men around that corral, and there were a handful of others lounging around the main house. None of them seemed particularly watchful, but that was probably a false impression, he knew. By now, Guerrero might be starting to wonder what had happened to the men he had sent to pick up the strangers to the south, strangers who had turned out to be himself and Buffalo and Rafael. Of course, Guerrero wouldn't know that.

Glancing up at the sun as it sank steadily toward the mountains, Daniels said, "If we do get the girls out without any trouble, what do we do about Guerrero then? We practically promised that priest we'd try to get rid of him."

"I been studyin' on that," Buffalo said solemnly.

"It'd be simple enough to ride on out of here if Guerrero didn't know the gals were gone, but he'd find out sooner or later and come lookin' for us. I don't cotton much to that idea." He glanced at the steep rock faces surrounding them and mused, "Wouldn't take a whole lot to make some of these boulders start fallin'."

"An avalanche?" Rafael asked. "It might catch us as well, Señor Buffalo."

Buffalo shrugged. "May have to take that risk if we're goin' to settle things with Guerrero. First things first, though."

Daniels nodded in agreement. And the first thing to do was wait until dark. . . .

Night fell in a hurry once the sun dropped behind the mountains. Daniels had observed that phenomenon before. One minute it was still light, then the next minute deep darkness cloaked the rugged landscape. He reached out, touched Buffalo's arm, and for some reason whispered as he asked, "Is it time?"

"Not just yet," Buffalo hissed back. "Listen!"

Daniels did, and he heard a faint clink of metal against rock. The sound was repeated a few seconds later, then was followed by a slight scraping noise. He frowned. What the devil . . . ?

Buffalo gestured toward the rim and whispered, "There's somebody climbin' up here."

Daniels breathed a heartfelt curse. There had been no guard around when they reached this spot, and they had decided that was because it would be so easy to see anyone who attempted to climb down the cliff. But now that night had fallen, Guerrero must have sent a man out to stand watch at the top of the man-made ladder.

If there was just one bandit, they could deal with him quietly enough. But if there was any kind of ruckus up here, that would draw attention to them and ruin their plan. Daniels held his breath as he peered around the edge of the boulder and waited to see how many men clambered over the rim.

A high-crowned sombrero came into view first, followed by the head and shoulders of the man wearing it.
He was cursing under his breath as he pulled himself
over the edge of the cliff and then stood up. There was
a rifle slung on his back. He unlimbered it and sighed,
no doubt dreading the prospect of another long, boring
night on guard duty. It was impossible to make out any
more details about him in this darkness.

Buffalo had brought the machete with him. Motioning
for Daniels and Rafael to stay still and quiet, he slid the
big blade out of its scabbard and started to stand up.

The bandit must have heard the slither of metal on
leather. He began to turn around just as Buffalo stepped
forward and swung the machete with all the power of
his burly form behind it.

Daniels heard a sound like the head of an ax smacking
into a chunk of wood. There was a rustle of clothes as
the guard slumped to the ground. Daniels looked around
the rock as Buffalo leaned over and wrenched the machete free from the dead man's skull.

Daniels blinked. He didn't even feel sick this time.
Maybe he was getting used to the killing. . . .

Buffalo took a quick glance over the rim and said
quietly, "Nobody else comin' up. Reckon this feller was
alone. We can start down now."

Daniels and Rafael got to their feet and joined Buffalo
at the edge. Buffalo took off his hat and poncho so they
wouldn't get in the way during the climb down, and
Daniels tossed his sombrero on the ground. Rafael said,
"You are sure you want me to stay here?"

"That's what I want," Buffalo nodded. "You ready,
Curtis?"

Daniels managed to nod. He was trying not to look
at the way the ground almost fell out from under his
feet. "I'm ready."

Turning his back to the cliff, Buffalo knelt and
reached behind him with one leg, letting it dangle in
midair as he searched for the first foothold. When he
found it, he moved down one more, then paused and

said to Daniels, "Give me a little start, then you come
on down. And don't fall; I'll be below you, and I don't
much feel like dodgin' you."

"Don't worry," Daniels said grimly. "I'll hang on."

"See that you do," Buffalo grunted. Then he disappeared beneath the rim.

Daniels leaned over so that he could watch Buffalo's
progress. When the big man was about ten feet below
the edge, Daniels knelt and followed him, groping with
the toe of his boot for the first notch. As he found it,
Rafael whispered, "Good luck, gringo."

Those were about the first civil words the Mexican
had had to say to him, Daniels thought. Better late than
never, he supposed. "And to you, too," he replied.
"Don't worry, Vasquez, we'll find your cousin."

He let his weight rest on the foothold and lowered
himself, feeling gingerly for the next one. His rapidly
beating heart felt like it was going to jump right up his
throat, and sweat beaded on his forehead.

Funny how a man never knew he was afraid of
heights until he tried to climb down a sheer cliff in pitch
blackness, Daniels thought.

Now that he was out here and hanging on for dear
life, there was no way he could look down and check
on Buffalo's progress. It seemed to Daniels that every
foot he covered took an hour. Buffalo should have ar-
rived at the bottom a long time ago. But that was only
an illusion, he told himself. Time wasn't really passing
that slowly. He hadn't been climbing down the cliff for
more than a few minutes.

His breath rasped in his throat as he lowered himself,
seeming so loud that surely everyone inside the stronghold must have heard it by now. No one was raising an
alarm, though. Daniels's fingers held tightly to the rock
as he reached down with his foot.

He had no idea how far he had come or how close he
was to the bottom. The very thought of turning his head
so that he could glance over his shoulder into the noth-
ingness behind and below him made his whole body

stiffen until he was afraid that he was not going to be able to move again. But then he forced his muscles to work, to take another step down.

An arm went around his midsection and a hand clapped itself over his nose and mouth. Daniels grunted in terror and tried to press himself even tighter against the cliff face. Instead he felt himself pulled away from the rock—and placed on solid ground.

"Dammit!" Buffalo Newcomb hissed in his ear. "You're down, you tarnal idjit! Now quit fightin' me!"

Daniels went limp with relief, and a second later, Buffalo removed the hand from his face. Drawing in a lungful of the clean, cool mountain air, Daniels felt like throwing himself down on the ground and never leaving it again. How the hell did birds stand it?

"You all right?" Buffalo asked.

Daniels nodded and stiffened his legs, which had been threatening to turn to jelly again. "I'm fine," he whispered. "What now?"

Buffalo touched his arm and then waved toward the house. "Come on."

The big man led the way, moving with that unlikely grace and silence of which he was capable at times. Daniels followed the flitting shadow, trying to be as quiet as he could. Every pebble he accidentally kicked sounded like an avalanche to him.

The stone house loomed closer. Buffalo and Daniels circled slightly so that their path lead them into the trees to one side of the building. The trees would give them some cover, and this route also took them away from the huts. Lights shone in a few of the small, rude structures, and the house itself was even more brightly lit. The yellow glow of lantern-light was visible through quite a few of the windows. Suddenly, as Daniels and Buffalo paused in the stygian darkness under the trees, the soft strains of a guitar came to their ears, followed by laughter.

Daniels frowned. He whispered, "Is Guerrero having a party?"

"Naw, that's just the usual Mexican celebratin'. They'll sing and pick a gee-tar and carry on for 'most any reason. You rode with Guerrero, you ought to know that."

"We never had much cause for celebrating," Daniels replied. "Things weren't going very well for Guerrero then. I guess his luck changed when he grabbed Doña Isabella."

"Reckon so. Well, come on. If we're lucky, they'll be knockin' back plenty of tequila, too, so they're liable to be a mite addlepated."

Daniels hoped Buffalo was right. They could use any advantage, no matter how small.

The trees ended a good twenty yards from the side of the house. They would have to cross that open ground to reach their objective. Daniels's nerves were jumping around crazily as he and Buffalo crouched at the edge of the trees.

"We'll just have to go fast and hope nobody sees us," Buffalo said. "You up to it?"

Daniels nodded, then realized Buffalo couldn't see that in the darkness. "I'm up to it," he said. "In fact, I'd just as soon get it over with."

"All right. When we get to the house, stick close to the wall and work your way around back. We'll see if we can find a likely lookin' window or door where we can get in."

With that, Buffalo straightened up and began to run toward the house. Daniels was close behind him, and again their footsteps and their breathing seemed abnormally loud to him. Buffalo reached the house and flattened himself against it. When Daniels got there, he leaned against the cold stone wall and clenched his jaw to keep from panting noisily. There was a little more light here, and he could see Buffalo as the big man began to slide along the wall and motioned for him to follow.

Daniels had been trying to think of where the girls might be held inside the house. If Guerrero was keeping

Isabella for himself, there was a good chance she and Angelina wouldn't be together. That would complicate matters, but there was nothing they could do about it. It figured that Guerrero would have the fanciest room in the house for himself, and Isabella might be there.

Buffalo crouched down to pass underneath a lighted window. As Daniels followed suit, a female voice coming from inside the room suddenly stopped him. He reached out, grasped Buffalo's shirt, and tugged on it urgently to stop the big man. As Buffalo swung around, Daniels put a finger to his lips and then gestured toward the window.

"Gracias, señorita," a man's voice said, and a woman replied, *"De nada."* A moment later, a door closed. There was a heavy sigh from inside the room.

Daniels and Buffalo waited in silence for a long moment. It appeared that the man had left the room, leaving the woman alone behind him. Of course, that might not be the case, but it was worth finding out, Daniels thought. He jerked a thumb toward the window and started to straighten.

Buffalo stopped him and gestured to his gun. Daniels nodded and slipped the pistol out of its holster, laying his thumb over the hammer so that he could cock it in a hurry if need be. Then he raised himself on his toes so that he could look through the opening.

There was a woman inside the little room on the other side of the window. She lay on a narrow bunk and wore a simple cotton shift. Her head was turned away from the window at the moment, but she did not seem to be asleep. Daniels could see her long, lustrous black hair. As he watched, she turned restlessly, bringing her features into view. He started to duck back down out of sight, then realized that her eyes were closed. She sighed again, evidently so tired that she couldn't decide whether or not to expend the energy required to get up and blow out the lantern.

Daniels's breath caught in his throat. The girl was beautiful, heartstoppingly lovely. He had seen her only for a few seconds back at the cantina, but he was not likely to ever forget her.

Angelina Vasquez...

Daniels dropped back into a crouch beside Buffalo. In an almost inaudible whisper, he said, "It's Angelina. She's alone. What do we do?"

Buffalo answered silently, pointing to the window, then to Daniels, then nodding emphatically. He concluded by holding his finger to his lips.

Daniels understood. Buffalo wanted him to go in there and get the girl, but silence was of the essence. If she was too startled, she might scream, and if she screamed, that would bring Guerrero's men.

Lacing his fingers together, Buffalo held them out like a stirrup to Daniels. The young Texan took a deep breath, holstered his gun, and then stepped into Buffalo's grip, reaching for the windowsill as he did so. With Buffalo boosting him, he hauled himself up and through the window.

It was impossible to do so without making some noise. The girl's eyes popped open, and Daniels could imagine what she was suddenly seeing—a gaunt, bearded, wild-eyed gringo in bloodstained peasant clothes, a pistol on his hip. He must have looked like something out of a nightmare.

She opened her mouth to scream.

Daniels flashed across the room, throwing himself on the bed and clamping a hand over her mouth. Her fists struck at him as she tried to writhe out from under him. He hissed desperately, "Angelina! Angelina, stop it! I'm a friend!"

Her eyes were still wide with terror above his callused hand, but her struggles eased a bit. He assumed he was getting through to her and pressed on urgently. "I've come to help you," he told her. "My friend and I are going to get you out of here, away from Guerrero! Your cousin Rafael is waiting for us."

That seemed to have more effect on her than anything else he had said so far. She stopped flailing at him and frowned. He could read the bafflement in her eyes. Leaning close to her so that his face was only a couple of inches from hers, he said, "If I take my hand away, will you promise not to scream or cry out? We don't want Guerrero to know that we're here."

Jerkily, Angelina nodded. After a second's hesitation, Daniels decided to believe her and lifted his hand from her face. She stared up at him and whispered, "Wh-who are you?"

"My name is Curtis Daniels," he told her. "My friend Buffalo and I have come to help you." He sat up so that his weight was no longer holding her down. "We'll get you out of here."

"You . . . you said my cousin . . . Rafael was here?"

"He's waiting with our mules on top of the cliff behind here. We've been trailing you ever since Guerrero kidnapped you from your father's cantina."

"Ah . . ." The exclamation of grief came out of her with a soft release of air. "My poor father and mother. *Dios*, how I have cried for them."

"I know. And I'm sorry. But there's no time now for anything except getting out of here."

She had to be boiling over with questions, wondering just who he was and why he was risking his life to rescue her. Obviously, she didn't remember him from the cantina as a member of Guerrero's band, or she wouldn't be feeling the trust he was starting to see in her eyes.

She caught at his sleeve as he stood up. "You said Buffalo, too."

"That's right, Buffalo Newcomb. He said he was a friend of your family."

"*Sí*, we knew Señor Buffalo. But Guerrero's men killed him."

Daniels shook his head. "It'll take more than a bunch of two-bit *bandidos* to kill Buffalo Newcomb." He held out his hand to her. "Come on, we don't have much time. Get your clothes on and we'll get out of here."

Angelina looked down at the shift with disgust. "My

other clothes were taken away. This would be all I needed, Guerrero said. He was right.''

Daniels was trying not to look at her breasts, the large, dark nipples visible through the thin fabric. He tried even harder not to think about what this girl must have been going through the past few weeks. Regardless of how bad it had been, though, her eyes shone with strength and fire. Her spirit had not been broken, despite what had been done to her body.

"We've got to go," he said gently. "We still have to get Doña Isabella out of here, too."

"You know about her?" Angelina asked as she stood up.

"We heard Guerrero was planning to marry her, that he had some crazy plan about getting his hands on her inheritance that way. She is still alive, isn't she?"

Angelina nodded. "She is alive in body, but that is all. The things she has seen, the idea of being married to a man like Guerrero, even against her will . . . It was too much for her, señor. Even though he has not laid a finger on her, her mind, it no longer works."

Daniels took a deep breath, trenches appearing in his lean cheeks. It was amazing how differently people reacted in times of trouble. Doña Isabella had lost her mind, even though she had not been physically harmed, while Angelina had been assaulted and degraded for weeks without snapping.

"Do you know where Guerrero is keeping her?"

"*Sí*, I can show you."

He led her to the window and handed her out to Buffalo, who wrapped his arms around her and hugged her tightly. "Lordy, gal, I was afraid we'd never see you again," he said quietly.

"Señor Buffalo," Angelina said, laying her head against his broad chest. "I thought you were dead. But I knew if anyone could save me, it would have to be someone like you."

"Not somebody like me, darlin'. You got the gen-u-ine article here."

"We'd better find Doña Isabella," Daniels said, hating to break up the reunion.

Angelina nodded. "This way—" she began.

A burst of raucous laughter made them draw back into the shadows against the wall. A group of men emerged from the darkness along the rear of the bench and came toward the house, pushing someone in front of them. The figure stumbled, righted itself, and then stepped into the glow cast from the rear door of the building. His captors were right behind him, guns ready.

Daniels breathed, "Damn," and stared from hiding at the now bloody face of Rafael Sebastiano y Roderigo Vasquez.

F O U R T E E N

THERE WAS A THIN trickle of crimson from one corner of Rafael's mouth, and his other cheek was scraped raw, as if he had been flung down on the rocks and had landed on his face. Obviously, he had put up a fight, but the odds against him had been too much for him to overcome.

"What the hell is he doin' here?" Buffalo hissed. "I told him to wait on top of the cliff!"

"Reckon he decided he didn't want to be left behind," Daniels replied in a whisper. His hand was on Angelina's arm, squeezing softly in a warning to be quiet. He was acutely aware of how her firm, warm flesh felt against his palm.

He was surprised there had been no shooting when Guerrero's men jumped Rafael. They must have spotted him coming down the cliff, Daniels thought, and grabbed him as soon as he reached the bottom.

Maybe they hadn't sent a man up the crude stone ladder to see if anyone else was lurking around. Maybe the mules were still up there . . .

Buffalo must have been thinking the same thing. As Rafael disappeared from view inside the house, the big man touched Daniels's arm and said, "You got to get the gal out o' here whilst you got the chance. Rafael's done fouled ever'thing up.''

"Rafael?" Angelina whispered. "That was Rafael?"

Daniels frowned. Didn't she recognize her own cousin?

There was no time to worry about that now. He turned to Buffalo and asked, "What are you going to do?"

"I'll sneak in and try to get that boy out of there, and Doña Isabella, too, if'n I can manage it. After what Angelina told us about her, though, I ain't sure she'd even notice bein' rescued. The two of you get out of here, 'n case things go bad.''

Daniels took a deep breath, trying to sort out the conflicting urges inside him. He did not want to leave Buffalo here to deal with Guerrero and the other bandits alone, but at the same time, he knew he had to get Angelina to safety. After all she had endured, it wouldn't be fair to ask her to risk any more. And somebody had to help Rafael, if it was at all possible. There was no real friendship between him and the Mexican, but they had ridden together, faced danger together, and there was no way he and Buffalo could leave Rafael to face Guerrero's wrath alone.

"All right," Daniels said, nodding abruptly. "I'll take Angelina up to the mules." He left it at that, undecided what he would do if he accomplished that much.

Buffalo clapped him on the shoulder. "Thanks, son," he rumbled. "I'll give you some time to get up the cliff 'fore I make my move. You watch sharp now, you hear? Could be some more of them *bandidos* up there waitin' for you.''

"I'll be careful," Daniels promised. He tightened his grip on Angelina's arm. "Come on."

The guitar had fallen silent, but there were still loud voices and laughter coming from inside the house. No screams as yet, Daniels thought, so Rafael wasn't being tortured. Guerrero would probably get around to it, though.

He forced those grim thoughts out of his mind and

looked around, peering through the shadows for any sign of movement. Seeing none, he pushed away from the wall and starting running for the trees, holding on to Angelina's arm and pulling her with him.

She wore no shoes, and he knew that running over the rocky ground had to be hell on bare feet. There was nothing they could do about it now. Better some cuts and bruises than slow death at the hands of the outlaws.

Breathless, they entered the trees and slowed to a halt. Daniels put one hand on the trunk of a tree for support and helped hold up Angelina with the other one. He drew in a couple of lungfuls of air, then said, "Are you all right?"

"S-sí," she panted. He waited for her to say something about her feet, but no more words came from her. After a moment, he said, "As soon as you're ready, we'll head for the cliff." He hoped he could find the handholds in the dark. Best to leave that worry unspoken, he decided. Angelina had to be terrified already, and there was no need to add to her fears.

She took a few deep breaths, then said, "I . . . I am ready, Señor Daniels."

"Curtis," he said, for some reason he couldn't quite fathom.

He sensed more than saw her nod. "Curtis," she repeated. "I am ready, Curtis."

With his hand on her arm again, they made their way through the trees, then hurried across the final stretch of open ground to the cliff. Daniels grimaced as they started along the base of the rock wall. He wished he had paid more attention to the way things had looked on the way down. He put out a hand, trailing the fingers along the stone above his head. If he overlooked the notches, maybe he would feel one and locate the path that way.

That was exactly what happened. His fingers encountered one of the notches. "Wait a minute!" he said to Angelina, then reached as high as he could with the other hand, trying to make sure that what he had felt wasn't some sort of natural gouge in the rock.

He found another handhold and knew he was in the right place. Leaning back, he stared up the cliff face. He could see the rim, a sharp edge of blackness with stars above it. As far as he could tell, there was nothing moving around up there.

"Give me your hand." He groped in the shadows for Angelina's outstretched fingers, found them, and placed them in one of the handholds. Crouching, he felt along the cliff for a spot where she could put her foot. He found one and whispered, "Here's a toehold. This won't be easy, especially since you don't have any shoes on, but you've got to do it, Angelina."

"I know that, Señor—Curtis. And I promise you, I would rather climb this cliff than go back there with Guerrero's men."

He heard the undercurrent of pain in her voice and wanted to comfort her, to take her in his arms and promise her that everything would be all right. He couldn't promise that, though, and he didn't know what else to do. So he said gruffly, "You go first. I'll be right behind you if you have any trouble. It's not far, only fifty feet or so."

"Sí." Angelina put her foot in the first notch, held on to the ones above her, and started to climb.

Only fifty feet or so, Daniels repeated to himself as he watched her pull herself up the cliff face. The white shift stood out against the dark rock, and he hoped that nobody down at the house glanced in this direction while they were climbing. Already his mouth was dry and his heart was thumping furiously in his chest. If not for Angelina, he might have rather faced Guerrero's men than make this climb again.

The girl pulled herself up another couple of feet, and Daniels knew it was time for him to start. He found a firm grip and began the ascent.

His muscles protested as he hauled his weight up the face of the cliff. The going was slow, even slower than it had been coming down. He could hear Angelina pant-

ing with effort. His own breath was hissing between
clenched teeth.

He looked up and saw her several feet above him. He
wanted to call out to her and ask her if she was all right,
but he didn't dare. Voices carried too well in this thin
mountain air. All of their conversation so far had been
conducted in soft whispers that wouldn't have been audible more than a few feet away.

They were more than halfway up the cliff, he guessed.
He wasn't just about to look down to make sure. Keep
going he told himself. Reach up, grab a handhold, pull,
reach up, grab another, pull . . .

A little dirt pattered down on his head, and he glanced
up in time to see Angelina scrambling over the rim. Only
a few more feet to go now, he realized. With a surge of
excitement, he lifted himself to the edge and pulled himself over.

Daniels rolled onto his back and took a deep breath,
then rolled again and came up into a crouch. Angelina
was waiting for him, about ten feet away from the edge.
Daniels's eyes searched the darkness, found the shapes
of the mules where they had been left. Evidently nothing
had disturbed them.

He had no idea what had prompted Rafael to ignore
Buffalo's orders and climb down the cliff. Obviously,
there had been no trouble up here.

Daniels hurried over to Angelina and pointed to the
mules. "You know how to ride?" he asked.

"I grew up on a rancho, Curtis," she said. "Of course
I know how to ride."

"Sure, I remember now." He led her over to the animals. "This is the mule I've been riding. He doesn't
have the most comfortable gait in the world, but he's
surefooted. He'll get you out of here all right. I want
you to take one of the pack mules, too, so you'll have
some supplies."

She put a hand on his arm. "You are not coming with
me?"

"I can't," he replied with a shake of his head. "I've

got to go back down there and help Buffalo and Rafael.''

Even as the words came out of his mouth, he realized that he hadn't made a conscious decision to return to Guerrero's stronghold. It was just something he had to do, he thought. From the day he had first joined Buffalo and Rafael in trailing the bandits, he had stopped running away from his troubles. He couldn't start again now.

''I do not understand who you are, Curtis Daniels, or why you are risking your life to help me, but . . . I am glad that you came to me.'' The girl moved slightly in the darkness, as if to touch him, then stopped. ''*Vaya con Dios,* Curtis.''

There were no hysterics, no pleading for him not to leave her alone here in the dark on top of a cliff, in some of the most rugged mountains on the face of the earth. No, she was worried about *him.*

Angelina Vasquez was quite a woman, Daniels thought.

''Don't worry, we'll catch up to you,'' he said. ''If you head east until you get to the edge of the mountains and then follow the foothills to the south, you'll come to that mission where Guerrero stopped. It's called San Cristóbal.''

''I remember.'' Her voice broke slightly. ''Guerrero shot the priest.''

''Father Vicente's all right,'' Daniels assured her. ''He was healing up when we came by the mission. The folks there will take care of you if we haven't caught up by then.''

He didn't say that if they had not appeared by the time she reached San Cristóbal, it was very likely they wouldn't be showing up in the future. She knew that as well as he did.

He could see her looking up at him in the starlight, and he gave in to an impulse. Putting his hand on the back of her neck, he drew her closer to him and gently kissed the top of her head. Then he said, ''We'd better both get going.''

Quickly, he turned and walked toward the cliff, knowing—just as he had during the climb up and down the sheer surface—that he didn't dare look behind him.

Buffalo Newcomb held the machete in his left hand and a pistol in his right as he catfooted along the wall toward the rear of the house. That was where the *bandidos* had taken Rafael. There was an entrance back there, and although it would probably be guarded, Buffalo was tired of sneaking around.

It was time to do what he did best: make sure that all hell broke loose.

There was a good chance that he and Rafael and Doña Isabella wouldn't get out of this alive. But Daniels and Angelina at least had a chance. They might be able to make it back to San Critóbal. What Daniels would do then, Buffalo didn't have any idea. He had a hunch the boy would wind up having to decide between two women, though, and that could be a heap worse than facing a bunch of bloodthirsty *bandidos*.

And Buffalo planned to make sure that Guerrero never got the chance to spend any more of his gold.

When he reached the corner of the big stone house, Buffalo paused and ventured a glance around it. Two men were lounging near the open doorway, smoking black cigars and talking in low voices. As Buffalo watched, another man appeared, spoke to the first two in tones quiet enough that Buffalo couldn't make out the words. But all three men disappeared inside the house.

Buffalo ducked around the corner. There was a staircase there that led up to the second floor. He climbed it quickly and at the top found a corridor leading to an inner balcony that ran all the way around the courtyard in the center of the building.

He had been lucky so far, damn lucky. It had to end sooner or later. But he was going to ride this horse as far as it would carry him.

The patio was large, with a few scrubby trees growing around a fountain in the middle of it. The fountain was dried up now, the sides of it beginning to crumble. It was just one more reminder of the time when this place must have been a home, rather than a hideout for bandits and renegades.

A lantern was burning at the far end of the courtyard. Ignacio Guerrero sat in a large wooden chair near the iron pole which held the lantern. The bandit chieftain was casually smoking a cigar and sipping from a glass of wine as he regarded the prisoner who stood in front of him.

Rafael held himself stiff and straight, refusing to acknowledge the danger in which he found himself. From the haughty look on the Mexican's face, Buffalo thought, Rafael might have been at one of the emperor's fancy parties back in Mexico City. He was flanked by two of Guerrero's men, and more outlaws stood behind him. All of their guns were holstered now, but there was an unmistakable feeling of menace in the air.

"So, Rafael," Guerrero said in a ringing voice that carried clearly to Buffalo's ears, "why have you decided to pay a visit to your old *compadre*?"

Buffalo frowned. What the hell did Guerrero mean by that?

Rafael spat toward Guerrero's boots. He was too far away to reach them, however, so all that got him was a smash across the back of the neck by the clubbed fists of one of Guerrero's men. Guerrero flipped a hand to call off his followers as Rafael stumbled forward under the impact of the blow.

Looking up at Guerrero, Rafael said harshly, "You are no *compadre* of mine. You are a dog who steals and betrays those who ride with him!"

Guerrero shrugged. "It was no fault of mine that the men decided they would rather have me for a leader than you, Rafael. You were too soft. You were more interested in smuggling than you were in making sure the reins of power were being held in an iron fist. As I hold them now . . ."

Crouched in the deep shadows along the balcony,

Buffalo gave a little shake of his head. "What them two Mexes're sayin' don't make a whole hell of a lot of sense," he muttered to himself.

But it became clearer as Guerrero went on. "After the men removed you as their leader two years ago, they turned to me for guidance. I was only too happy to provide it."

"Of course!" Rafael said bitterly. "It was you who spoke against me behind my back, you who turned loyal men against me. You who were my trusted lieutenant!"

"Perhaps, but look around you, my friend. You see a prosperity that the group never knew in the days when you led us. Then, we never had a home like this."

Rafael laughed humorlessly. "I have heard about your 'prosperity,' Guerrero. Until just a few weeks ago, you were nothing but a minor bandit, a mere annoyance. Yes, you have this place—because no one else wants it. And how long do you think you will hold it?"

Guerrero blew smoke into the air. "I can defend this stronghold against anything short of an army. And there are no armies in the Sierra Madre. The emperor's troops and the *Juaristas* are too busy fighting each other."

"Sooner or later, though, the revolution will be over. And then whichever side is the victor will crush you!"

"You will not be alive to see that day, Rafael," Guerrero said solemnly. He slid his revolver out of its holster. "You will be long dead by then, *compadre*."

Buffalo had been slipping along the balcony while Guerrero and Rafael talked, but he had still heard enough of the conversation for a few things to start making sense. He could puzzle it all out later—if he was still alive. If he wasn't . . .

Well, then, there wasn't any point in worrying about it, was there?

Guerrero was just about to pull back the hammer of his pistol when a hairy apparition leaped from the balcony to his right, howling and landing on top of two of his men. The machete flickered in the lanternlight, and a sombreroed head seemed to leap from the shoulders beneath it.

And the worst thing about it was—the monster began to sing.

Buffalo whirled, wielding the heavy machete with deadly accuracy. At the same instant, he began to fire the gun in his other hand. It bucked against his palm as the blasts roared from it and men fell crazily, spilled by the bullets. Buffalo bellowed out a bawdy song about a widow named Kathleen. He chopped another man down with the machete and looked for Guerrero.

Guerrero had sprung to his feet as soon as he recovered from the shock of Buffalo's entrance. That gap lasted only seconds, but it was long enough for Rafael to throw himself forward. Rafael's hands had not been tied; after all, how much trouble could he cause while he was surrounded by Guerrero's men?

Lashing out, Rafael knocked Guerrero's gun aside and barreled into the bandit. They staggered into the chair where Guerrero had been sitting, overturning it and tangling their legs with the chair's. Both men went down.

Buffalo felt a slug burn across his shoulder but ignored the pain. He thrust out with the machete, driving the blade into a man's stomach and then using it to haul the *bandido* around in front of him as a shield. Several bullets thudded into the man's body, finishing the job that the machete had started. The bandit sagged toward Buffalo.

The big man let out another howl. He had spied his Arkansas Toothpick sheathed on the dead man's hip. Leaving the machete where it was—driven completely through the bandit's body so that the point protruded from his back—Buffalo grabbed the familiar hilt of the big knife and jerked it free. He would die with an old friend in his hand, by God!

And it looked like that was exactly what was about to happen, because there were at least a dozen of Guerrero's men spilling into the courtyard, all of the bandits bristling with weapons and ready to use them.

The hammer of Buffalo's gun clicked on an empty chamber. He was out of bullets, with no time to reload. He glanced over his shoulder, his attention drawn by the sound of a struggle, and saw Rafael and Guerrero each trying to choke the life out of the other one. The bandits paused as well, shocked by the scene of battle, but then they surged forward again toward the big, bearded man.

"Reckon it's time to write the last verse in 'The Ballad of Buffalo Newcomb,' " he said with a grin, waiting for them.

F I F T E E N

THE CLIMB BACK DOWN the cliff was a blur to Daniels. Just as before, he had no idea he was near the bottom until his boots hit the rocky surface of the bench. With both feet on solid ground, he stood there for a moment with his hands on the cliff, leaning against it while he caught his breath and tried to slow his racing pulse.

The shooting and yelling made him jerk away from the rock wall.

If there was that big a ruckus going on, Buffalo had to be involved. No need to keep quiet now. Daniels yanked his gun from its holster and ran toward the house.

A couple of men emerged from one of the huts as he passed it. They must have thought he was one of them at first, because they kept running, but then the realization that he was tall and blond hit them. They twisted around, bringing up the rifles they carried.

Daniels shot them both.

He aimed and fired without thinking and was barely aware that they had gone spinning to the ground. Then he was past them, reaching back to pull cartridges from his shell belt and replacing the spent ones on the run.

There was an open door in the rear of the house. Daniels headed for it, unsure of where it would lead but knowing that there would be trouble wherever he wound up. For an instant, as he bounded into the building, a wave of sickness rippled through him. More blood, more killing . . . Was it ever going to stop?

Not any time soon, he saw as he threw himself to the floor of the corridor. The man who had appeared in front of him fired wildly. Daniels triggered a single shot from his prone position. The bullet caught the *bandido* in the stomach and drove him back into the room from which he had emerged.

Daniels scrambled to his feet. He could hear singing now and knew that had to be Buffalo. The sound was coming from somewhere in the center of the big building. Daniels kept going in that direction.

He came out into a large courtyard in time to see a mass of men charging toward Buffalo. Several men were already down, felled by bullets or machete blows. Daniels skidded to a stop, raised the gun in his hand, and started firing.

The slugs smashed into Guerrero's men from behind. At the same time, Buffalo took the battle to the enemy, wading in with the Arkansas Toothpick. Daniels emptied the Colt, then flung it aside and snatched up a pair of rifles that had been dropped by their now-dead owners. He fired both of them.

On the other side of the courtyard, Rafael and Guerrero were still grappling. Daniels caught a glimpse of them through the haze of powder smoke floating in the air, saw Guerrero fling Rafael off him. The bandit chieftain rolled over, his hand darting out to pick up a knife.

Rafael spotted the hilt of the machete sticking up from the body of the man Buffalo had cast aside. He dove for it, yanking it free of the corpse. As he turned, Guerrero came up on one knee facing him. The bandit's arm flashed forward, the knife spinning across the gap between them.

With a grunt, Rafael staggered a step back. The blade had caught him high in the left side, just below the shoulder. Guerrero had been aiming for the heart, but his throw had not gone true. With a high-pitched cry, a mixture of pain and triumph, Rafael thrust the machete out in front of him and threw himself forward.

The big blade ripped through Guerrero's body, adding more blood to the slippery film that already covered it. Guerrero screamed as he went over backward, borne down by the force of Rafael's blow. Crimson sprayed from his open mouth.

Crouched above him, Rafael ripped the machete from side to side, both hands wrapped around the hilt. The pain from his own wound hit him then, and he sagged there, holding himself up with the machete. Sweat dripped from his face and fell onto Guerrero's bulging eyes, which were now staring sightlessly into the flames of hell.

The king of the Sierra Madre was dead.

Daniels and Buffalo had fought their way through the knot of bandits until they were back-to-back. Now, suddenly, the men who had been trying to kill them a second before were lowering their weapons and backing off. Daniels looked over, saw Rafael painfully pulling himself to his feet and standing over Guerrero's body. Rafael reached down, grasped the hilt of the machete, and pulled it free. He turned, a fierce smile on his face, and lifted his other hand to yank the knife from his own body. He tossed that blade aside contemptuously.

"The fighting is over," he announced, his voice carrying through the courtyard.

"What . . . ?" Daniels muttered, unsure what was happening.

"Heard an old sayin' once," Buffalo said, wiping blood from a cut on his forehead. "Went like this: 'The king is dead. Long live the king. . . . ' "

Rafael was like a different man now, barking orders and having the dead bodies hauled out of the courtyard. Men who had been his captors less than an hour earlier now followed his commands without complaint. Daniels stared at what was going on, part of his mind refusing

to believe it. Surely the battle would start again at any
second.

"I don't understand any of this," he said to Buffalo.

The big man was binding up a gash on his forearm.
"Trial by combat," he grunted. "Didn't start out like
that, but that's the way it ended up. Rafe killed Guerrero,
so he's got the right to take over what's left of Guerrero's gang."

"You're talking like Rafael's a bandit, too."

Buffalo was sitting on the wall around the old fountain. He looked up shrewdly at Daniels. "Reckon he
probably is. I heard him an' Guerrero talkin' 'fore the
fightin' started. Seems the two of 'em used to ride together. Fact is, Rafe was the leader of the bunch then.
Guerrero took over, and I reckon Rafe had to light out
to save his own hide. When he found out that we were
goin' after Guerrero, he figgered this was his chance to
get back at the bastard. That's why he wanted to come
along and help us."

"But what about Angelina? She really is his cousin,
isn't she?"

" 'Spose so," Buffalo shrugged. "But I'd be willin'
to bet Rafe weren't too interested in gettin' her back. He
planned on us distractin' Guerrero and his men by tryin'
to rescue them gals. Whilst that was goin' on, he could
sneak in here and kill Guerrero. Didn't quite work out
that way, but Guerrero wound up dead anyway."

Daniels shook his head, not sure if Buffalo's theory
made any sense or not. It was possible, he supposed.

Rafael strolled over to them. The wound in his shoulder had been bandaged, and while he was a little pale,
there was a cocky smile on his face. *"Compadres!"* he
greeted them. "Are either of you badly hurt?"

"Reckon we'll live," Buffalo replied. "Just a few
nicks and scrapes here and there. What about you?"

"I am fine, Señor Buffalo. Just fine."

Daniels said, "From the looks of things, I'd say
you've taken over here."

"Sí," Rafael nodded. "Some of these men know me

from the old days, and others have heard of me. Now that Guerrero is dead by my hand, they are willing to follow me.''

Buffalo inclined his head toward the bandits who were cleaning up the mess in the courtyard. ''You sure you can trust these fellers?''

''Of course.''

Rafael looked very pleased with himself, Daniels thought. But Guerrero had replaced him as the leader of the gang once before, and now Rafael had overthrown Guerrero in turn.

Sooner or later, some other bandit would get ambitious and try to wrest control of the group from Rafael. Daniels felt a touch of pity as he thought that Rafael didn't realize he would be spending the rest of his life looking over his shoulder.

''If it's all right with you, Rafael, I'll go up and get Angelina,'' Daniels said. ''I told her to take a couple of mules and head east, but she hasn't had time to get very far.''

''Certainly. It will be good to see my cousin again.''

''I'll stay here,'' Buffalo said to Daniels. He put his hand on the hilt of the Arkansas Toothpick. ''Already found part of what Guerrero's bunch stole from me. I'd like to see if I can scout up my Dragoon and my Sharps, too.''

Daniels nodded and started out of the courtyard, keeping a wary eye on Guerrero's men. Rafael's men now, he thought. That would take some getting used to. Obviously, the impression Rafael gave of belonging to the upper classes was just part of a facade.

Daniels took a deep breath as he approached the cliff. It seemed as if he had been going up and down this rock wall all night. With any luck, though, he would only have to do it once more. When it came time to retrieve the mules, they could go down to the other end of the valley and circle around the long way.

It was easier to find the handholds this time. He began to climb and found that he wasn't as frightened, either.

For a change, the ascent went quickly, and when he pulled himself over the rim, he was able to stand up right away without having to lie there and recover his composure first.

He stopped short as a shape loomed out of the darkness. He saw the upraised hands and the rock they clutched and knew that it was aimed at his head. His hand flashed toward the gun on his hip.

But then he cried out suddenly, "Don't, Angelina! It's me, Curtis!"

She let out a startled gasp and dropped the rock. Then she was in his arms, her face pressed against his chest, sobs shaking her body. "I . . . I thought you were one of Guerrero's men!" she said raggedly. "I heard the shooting and yelling. . . . I knew you all had to be dead. . . ."

"Not hardly," he said, grinning and clumsily stroking her long, black hair. "Buffalo and I are just fine, and so's your cousin Rafael."

Angelina straightened and looked up at him. The moon had risen, and he could see her face in its silvery glow. "I still do not understand about Rafael," she said. "None of us had seen him for years. He . . . he was thrown out of the army for stealing, and then we heard that he was some sort of smuggler. . . . How did he happen to be with you?"

"He came along right after Guerrero raided your folks' place. I reckon from what I've heard tonight that he was probably down on his luck and thought maybe he could get some food and a place to stay because of the fact that he was family. That's just a guess." Daniels shrugged, well aware that his arms were still around her and that she wore only the shift. "Things happen, and we don't always know the reason for them."

"*Sí* . . ."

Daniels hesitated a moment, then said, "Why didn't you take the mules and light out, like I told you to?"

"I wanted to wait and see what happened. I . . . I could not bear the thought of leaving you and Señor

Buffalo down there like that. Will you forgive me for disobeying you, Curtis?''

He wanted to laugh. There was nothing to forgive. He said, ''Come on. You must be cold. The fighting's all over, so we'll go down and get you some clothes.''

''We must climb down the cliff again?''

''Just one more time,'' he promised her.

By the time they reached the house, the tension that had been keeping Angelina from noticing the cold had eased enough so that she was shivering. Buffalo Newcomb met them, and he had a blanket in his hands.

''Figgered you might need this,'' he said gruffly, handing the blanket to Angelina. ''Wrap up an' get warm, gal. It's been a long night.''

That was the truth, Daniels thought. It was all starting to catch up with him, too. Even as leery as he was of lying down in what had been the house of his enemy, he had to admit that the idea of a nice, soft bed sounded mighty good.

''Rafael wants to see you,'' Buffalo went on to the girl.

''All right,'' she said noncommittally as she draped the blanket around her shoulders.

Buffalo led them through the house to a large room next to the patio. A window looked out over the courtyard, and Daniels could see in the lanternlight that except for some bloodstains on the flagstones, all signs of the carnage that had occurred there were gone. He wondered briefly what had been done with Guerrero's body. It was no doubt piled somewhere with all the other corpses.

The chair in which Guerrero had been sitting outside had been carried into this room, and Rafael occupied it now. He didn't get up as Daniels, Buffalo, and Angelina entered, but he gave them a languid smile. From his negligent pose, one elbow on the arm of the chair and that hand propping up his chin, he was taking this ''king of the Sierra Madre'' business seriously. He certainly looked like a man who had just dethroned royalty and taken its place.

"Angelina!" he said. "Dear cousin! It is so good to see you. You are unharmed?"

"*Sí*," she nodded.

"It has been a long time, has it not?"

"Many years," Angelina replied.

Buffalo looked a little puzzled by her attitude, which stopped just short of outright hostility. Daniels could understand it a little better, and he would have to explain the situation to the big man later. For now he just caught Buffalo's eye and gave a tiny shake of his head.

"I truly regret the evil that Guerrero visited on you, my cousin," Rafael went on. "I know that there is no way to make it up to you, but I will do what I can. I have decided that we will have a fiesta! All the people of the valley will attend. I want them to see that the days of Guerrero's tyranny are at an end."

That so-called tyranny had lasted only a couple of weeks, Daniels thought, but he didn't say anything. If Rafael wanted to have a party, that was his business.

"The three of you will come, too, of course. This is the dawning of a new day, my friends. . . ."

Daniels wasn't sure he wanted to hang around for the fiesta. Maybe it was time for him to ride on, to resume his life of drifting. He knew he didn't want to stay here permanently. Rafael might not be the butcher that Guerrero had been, but he obviously intended to resume his former life as a bandit. That was something Daniels could never do.

Angelina broke into his musing by asking, "Has anyone thought to check on Doña Isabella?"

Daniels glanced at Buffalo, saw the big man shrug. "We all been a mite busy," Buffalo said.

"Come on." Daniels took Angelina's arm, grateful for the fact that the blanket was covering her bare flesh now. "Do you know where her room is?"

"*Sí*," Angelina nodded. "I will show you."

Rafael finally got to his feet. "Yes, I will accompany

you as well. I must tell the lady what has happened and make her aware that she is no longer in any danger.''

''Plannin' on sendin' her back to her family?'' Buffalo asked as they walked down a corridor, following Angelina.

''Naturally. Of course, I will expect to be handsomely rewarded for performing such a service. I have others to think of besides myself now. A responsibility to my men . . . You understand.''

Daniels understood, all right. Rafael was rapidly turning into as big an outlaw as his predecessor. He was planning to sell Doña Isabella back to her family for ransom, the very idea he had been horrified by when Buffalo suggested it.

He was going to be glad when he was away from here, Daniels thought.

Angelina paused in front of door and rapped on it. ''Doña Isabella,'' she called softly. ''It is Angelina Vasquez. Do not be afraid, señora. Some friends have come to help us. Doña Isabella, do you hear me?''

There was no response from inside.

Angelina turned to the three men and said, ''It is as I feared. She does not answer because she can no longer hear us. She has retreated too far into her fear for simple words to reach her.''

Rafael gestured curtly at the door. ''Open it. We must be sure that she is all right otherwise.''

Angelina nodded, grasped the latch, and turned it. The door swung open under her touch.

She gasped as she looked inside, then turned away quickly, her face pale. Without thinking about what he was doing, Daniels took her in his arms again. Obviously, she had just seen something that had severely shaken her.

He peered over her shoulder. In the faint light from a lantern that was about to go out, he saw Doña Isabella Alvarez dangling from one of the ceiling beams, strips of material torn from her dress knotted together and then placed around her neck. There was no doubt that she was dead.

Rafael cursed fervently, seeing his dreams of ransom money evaporating. Buffalo's face was grim as he said, "She must've heard all the fightin' an' shootin', and it was finally too much for her. I'm a mite surprised she didn't take this way out 'fore now."

"*Dios mio,*" Angelina said, still pressed against Daniels. "That poor woman . . ."

As sorry as he was for Doña Isabella, Daniels thought, "that poor woman" hadn't had nearly as many bad things happen to her as Angelina had. And yet Angelina was still holding together. She was strong, all right, strong as well as beautiful.

"I will have my men attend to her," Rafael said, still looking bleakly at the body of Doña Isabella. He turned away, and the smile reappeared on his face. "Now come, my friends. It has been a trying night, and we all need to rest."

The four of them went back down the corridor, leaving the door open behind them.

S I X T E E N

BUFFALO SCRATCHED THE COARSE, gray fur on Stink's back and said, "You can say what you want 'bout ol' Rafe, but he sure knows how to throw a party."

That was true, Daniels thought. The place was crowded with merrymakers. All the farmers in the valley had come, bringing food and wine with them. After all, who was going to refuse an invitation from the man who killed Ignacio Guerrero?

It was the second day since the night of Guerrero's death. The previous day had been spent burying the dead, including Guerrero himself and Doña Isabella. The word had gone out then that Rafael was having a fiesta, and early that morning, the celebrants had begun to arrive.

Daniels, Angelina, and Buffalo were sitting in the courtyard, on the low wall around the fountain. Daniels remembered Buffalo sitting in the same spot to bind up his wounds. Many of the villagers were dancing on the patio, the music provided by men with guitars and fiddles, some of them bandits, some farmers. For today, at least, there was peace in this valley.

But it wouldn't last, Daniels told himself. Maybe he was being too pessimistic, he thought, but he believed that sooner or later Rafael would decide that Guerrero had had the right idea.

The king is dead....

Angelina was wearing a brilliant red skirt and a white blouse, and Daniels thought she was the loveliest thing he had ever seen. There was a question he wanted to ask her, but so far he hadn't seemed to be able to find the right moment for it.

Buffalo was wearing his Arkansas Toothpick again, and on his other hip rode the Dragoon Colt he had been carrying for years. He had found it, along with his Sharps, among the effects of some of the bandits who had been killed. The heavy carbine was leaning against the fountain wall beside him. He had reclaimed his hat and poncho as well and now looked much the same as he had the first time Daniels saw him. It was hard to believe that had been less than a month earlier. Sometimes he felt as if he had known Buffalo Newcomb all his life. The big man had that effect on people.

Daniels had found his sombrero atop the cliff, and he wore it now, although the high-crowned hat was pushed onto his back, held there by the thong around his throat. He watched the dancing and listened to the music and enjoyed the feel of the warm sunshine on his face. Under the circumstances, he should have been happier than he was, he thought. But things kept gnawing at him....

Angelina laid a soft hand on his arm. "You look unhappy, Curtis. Is there anything I can do ... ?"

He looked up, his gaze meeting her eyes as he came to an abrupt decision. He should have known by now that he couldn't postpone the unpleasant things in his life. Better to get them over with.

"Why don't we take a walk?" he asked.

"Of course. Or if you would rather dance—"

"Nope. I'd like to find someplace quieter, in fact."

Angelina flushed slightly. She looked over at the big bearded man and said, "Señor Buffalo, you will accompany us?"

He shook his head. "I ain't no blamed *mamacita*, gal.

You don't need a chaperone with Curtis, here. He's only a mite dangerous. Most of the time, he's plumb harmless.''

Daniels snorted, unsure if he had been complimented or insulted. "Come on," he said, taking Angelina's hand.

She went with him, and he led her to an alcove off the courtyard. The music was still plainly audible, but at least there was not as much celebrating going on all around them. The fiesta was centered at the other end of the patio, where Rafael seemed to be attempting to dance with every female in the valley over the age of twelve.

"Your cousin's enjoying himself," Daniels commented when they were alone.

"*Sí*. Rafael has always wanted this sort of power. Now he has it."

"And you don't trust him, do you?"

Angelina shook her head solemnly. "No, Curtis, I do not. I would like to leave this place."

"That's what I was going to ask you, what you were planning to do now."

"I do not know. But I cannot stay here."

Daniels could understand that. This place held too many bad memories. Not only that, but some of the men who had survived the battle two nights previously were ones who had raped her during her captivity. Neither of them could stay, Daniels thought, because if he tried to, he would wind up trying to kill the sons of bitches.

"Where would you like to go?"

"I . . . I thought about San Cristóbal." She lowered her eyes, then asked, "Will you take me there?"

Daniels had been afraid she would ask that of him. He had vowed not to go back there, but he couldn't refuse Angelina.

"I'll take you," he said softly, "but I can't stay there myself."

She looked up in surprise. "But why not? I am sure the padre would not mind, and the villagers are good people. They would make you welcome.''

"I know that. But I can't stay anywhere for very long, Angelina. I've got to keep moving. . . .''

"Why?'' she asked, obviously upset by what he was saying.

He took a deep breath and met the level stare she was now giving him. "I'm on the run, Angelina,'' he said. "I'm wanted for murder and robbery in Texas.''

Her eyes widened for a moment, but then she said, "I do not care. This is Mexico, not Texas. You are safe here.''

"From the law, maybe.''

"What do you mean?''

"I killed my wife,'' he said flatly. "A man can't escape from that.''

She breathed a prayer, shocked by what he had just told her. After a moment, she said, "I . . . I'm sure you . . . you had a reason. . . .''

"Oh, I had a reason, all right,'' Daniels said, not looking at her now. He squinted into the bright sunlight, seeing not Mexico but Texas, seeing the horrible scene that had met his gaze when he came in from working in the fields on that day.

He saw his wife, his beautiful Willa, waving a bloody butcher knife over the body of their son Matt. He saw their daughter Callie huddled in a corner, terrified. He watched as Willa turned away from the boy and leaped toward Callie, the light of madness burning like fire in her eyes. The butcher knife lifted in Willa's hand, Callie screamed—

And Curtis Daniels fired the rifle in his hand.

The words came out of him somehow, explaining the life of a hardscrabble farmer, the hunger and the difficulties of a bad year followed by another and another and another. And then the wind on top of that, the Texas wind that blew all the time and took the arid land—and anything else that was good—away with it. It had taken Willa's sanity. She had murdered Matt and had been about to slaughter Callie as well.

Daniels had done the only thing he could to save his daughter's life. He had put a bullet through Willa's brain.

"She didn't kill Callie," he heard himself saying to Angelina, "but she might as well have. The poor little girl was so scared, she never got over it. I took her to some of our neighbors, so that they could take care of her, and then I lit out. I couldn't stand to stay around there. Everywhere I looked, I saw things that reminded me of Willa and the way I had let her down. It was my fault, all my fault. I never should have asked them to live like that. . . .

"Well, I stayed in touch with the folks who were taking care of Callie. I sent them money for her, whenever I could come up with any. I guess . . . I guess that's when I became an outlaw. It didn't seem like I was doing anything wrong, though. I just wanted to take care of my little girl. I heard from them that she never recovered from what had happened, that she just sat and rocked in a little rocking chair and never played or helped out or anything, never even said much. I couldn't go back and face that, even if I hadn't been on the wrong side of the law by then.

"But then I heard that the sheriff had decided that I must have killed Willa and Matt both. He was charging me with murder, making me out to be some kind of monster. That's when I headed for the Rio and crossed into Mexico. I . . . I don't know how Callie's doing now, or even if she's still alive. Maybe I am safe on this side of the border, I don't know. But I can't stay in one place, can't settle down. If I did, then sooner or later, I . . . I'd hurt the people around me."

She had listened to his story in silence. Now, as his voice trailed off, she reached out, took his hand. Her fingers twined with his. "I am so sorry," she whispered. "So much pain . . . But you are wrong, Curtis. You cannot carry that pain around with you for the rest of your life. You can let go of some of it. You can share it."

"How?"

Angelina took a deep breath. "I have much pain, too. We can carry all of it . . . together." She smiled, a sad smile but one touched with hope at the same time. "We will go back to San Cristóbal. Then . . . we will see."

Daniels felt himself nodding. Already, there was a strange peace stealing over him, a calmness unlike any he had felt in a long time. "Yes," he said. "We'll see."

With her hand still in his, they walked back toward the center of the courtyard. Buffalo wasn't sitting by the fountain anymore, Daniels saw. In fact, there was no sign of the big man anywhere.

"Wonder where Buffalo's got off to?" he murmured, more to himself than to Angelina. "Maybe Rafael saw him leave—"

"There is Señor Buffalo," Angelina said suddenly. She pointed.

Buffalo emerged from the house and started to cross the courtyard toward the front entrance. He had a pair of saddlebags over his shoulder, and he was carrying the bag in which Stink rode. Daniels looked past him, through the arched, wrought iron gate that led out of the courtyard and through a short passage to the outside. Buffalo's saddle mule and one of the pack mules were waiting there.

Daniels frowned. What the hell was going on? Did Buffalo intend to leave without even saying good-bye?

Somebody else had noticed him among the crowd. The music abruptly fell silent as Rafael called out, "Señor Buffalo! Where are you going, amigo?"

Buffalo stopped and turned slowly. He was grinning. "Don't want you to think I'm runnin' out on your little fiesta, Rafe, but I just figgered it was time for a fiddle-footed ol' codger like me to be movin' on."

Rafael walked toward him, the partygoers hurriedly getting out of his way. He was wearing a fine, expensive suit that had once been Guerrero's, his hair was sleekly combed, and the only thing marring his appearance was the sling supporting his left arm.

And the ugly expression in his eyes, Daniels thought.

He squeezed Angelina's hand and said quietly, "Come on. Something's up."

They made their way through the crowd, closing in on Buffalo from a different angle and arriving at his side at the same moment as Rafael. With a smile on his lips that didn't reach his eyes, Rafael gestured at the saddlebags slung over Buffalo's shoulder and said, "I hope you have plenty of provisions, *compadre*."

"Oh, sure," Buffalo nodded. "Don't worry about that."

"And ammunition and powder for your weapons," Rafael went on. "We have plenty stored in one of the huts."

"I know. Just paid a visit to it. I figgered you wouldn't mind me outfittin' myself."

Rafael waved a hand. "Of course not. You and I have ridden the long trails together, Señor Buffalo. What is mine is yours."

"Well, that's mighty neighborly of you—" Buffalo began.

Rafael cut him off by sliding his gun out of its holster. "Except the gold," he said, the smile dropping off his face and his voice becoming as cold as his gaze. "The gold is now mine."

Daniels tensed. He didn't know what gold Rafael was talking about, but obviously Buffalo did. The big man said quietly, "Don't do this, Rafe."

Daniels spoke up. "Look, Rafael, I don't know what this is about, but if Buffalo wants to leave I think you should let him. After all, he did save your life."

"Be quiet, gringo," Rafael snapped. "This is none of your affair. If Newcomb wants to leave, no one will stop him—as long as he hands over those saddlebags."

"Can't do that, Rafe," Buffalo said, and he sounded genuinely regretful. "Folks keep tryin' to take this gold away from me. I'm gettin' a mite tired of it."

"Then you are a fool. You cannot hope to fight your way out of here. Now give me the gold!"

Buffalo ignored him. He glanced at Daniels and said, "You and Angelina with me, Curtis?"

Daniels wore a deep frown of confusion. "I guess so," he said. "I'm still not sure—"

"Good," Buffalo cut in. " 'Cause I got a idea it ain't goin' to be too healthy round here—"

The explosion seemed to shake the whole world.

Daniels grabbed Angelina as the blast rocked the bench where the house sat. She screamed, but her cry was lost among the dozens of other startled screams. Rafael cursed and thumbed back the hammer of his pistol as he lifted it.

Seeing the threat out of the corner of his eye, Daniels acted without thinking. He kicked at Rafael's hand, his foot catching the Mexican on the wrist and knocking the gun aside as Rafael pulled the trigger. The shot went wild, and in the next instant Buffalo Newcomb's Dragoon crashed. Rafael was thrown backward by the heavy ball smashing into his uninjured shoulder.

Another deafening explosion assaulted their ears as Buffalo jammed his pistol back in its holster, grabbed Angelina's other arm, and yelled, "Come on!"

The big courtyard was a mass of confusion now. Near the house, a column of dust and smoke rose toward the clear blue sky, and gravel pattered down everywhere. Daniels, Buffalo, and Angelina ran toward the entrance, leaving behind them a writhing and cursing Rafael. "Damn you, Newcomb!" he shrieked after them. "You will pay for this! You cannot do this to—"

That was the last Daniels heard, the frantic commotion drowning out the rest of Rafael's threats. There were bandits everywhere, but none of them seemed to know for sure what had happened. The dozens of villagers from the valley added to the confusion.

Buffalo thundered through the shady arched entranceway and out into the sunlight again. Daniels and Angelina were right behind him. Buffalo waved a hand at the path leading to the valley and shouted, "Down there! Grab some horses!"

Daniels did as he was told, hanging on to Angelina and running toward the trail. He heard shots behind him and glanced back to see Buffalo trading lead with a few of the *bandidos* who had followed them out of the house. The fire from the Dragoon drove Rafael's men behind cover.

Angelina was panting beside him as they ran. Well, Daniels thought wryly, neither one of them had wanted to stay around here anyway. And now they couldn't for sure, since Rafael had turned on Buffalo and they had found themselves allied with the big man.

The steep path made for difficult running, but Daniels and Angelina managed. When they reached the bottom, Daniels saw that there was no one around the corral. The horses were milling around nervously, shaken up by the explosions. There would not be time to saddle any of them, Daniels knew. He and Angelina would have to ride bareback.

"Here comes Señor Buffalo!" she cried, looking back while he swung the corral gate open.

Daniels glanced at the path up the cliff and saw Buffalo riding down it on the mule, leading the pack animal behind him. They were going too fast for that slope; the haunches of the mules were almost on the ground. But somehow Buffalo kept them on their feet and moving.

There were hackamores hanging on the fence. Daniels grabbed a couple and moved into the corral. He had never been a great judge of horseflesh, but he picked out a couple of likely looking animals and slipped the rawhide bridles on them. The hackamores would beat nothing.

"Let's go!" Buffalo shouted as he reached the bottom of the trail and sent his mule galloping toward the corral. Daniels held the lines of both horses and boosted Angelina onto the back of one of them. Then he vaulted onto the other one and tugged its head around.

"Follow Buffalo!" he told the girl.

"Curtis! What are you going to do?"

He slapped Angelina's mount across the rump and

sent it lunging after Buffalo's mule. "Just go!" he called out to her.

As Buffalo and Angelina rode down the valley, Daniels whipped his hat off and sent his mount among the other horses. He began whooping and slapping at the horses with his big sombrero. Some of the frightened animals stampeded through the open gate. Others pressed against the rails of the corral until the wood split and collapsed. Within seconds, the *bandidos'* horses were galloping crazily away from the cliffs.

A bullet sang past Daniels's head. He banged his heels against the flanks of his own mount and raced after Buffalo and Angelina. They had a head start on him, but he closed the gap quickly. He caught up with Angelina first, then Buffalo slowed slightly until they both drew even with him.

"Smart thinkin'!" the big man called to Daniels over the thunder of hoofbeats. "It'll take 'em a while to round up them horses!"

Daniels nodded. He looked over at Angelina, who seemed a little pale but otherwise all right. What had started as a fiesta had ended up as a free-for-all, but somehow the three of them had come through it without any fresh injuries. Even the possum seemed to be all right. Buffalo had tied the bag to his saddle horn, as usual, and Stink's nose and tail were protruding from the usual openings.

Looking back over his shoulder as they galloped away from the stronghold, Daniels saw Rafael's men scurrying this way and that as they tried to capture some of the spooked horses. A few of them pointed rifles at the fleeing trio. Daniels saw puffs of smoke from the weapons, but the range was already too great. They were going to get away.

But from what and to where? Those were the questions that still needed answers.

S E V E N T E E N

DANIELS REINED IN AND looked over at Buffalo New-comb. "All right, what the hell happened back there?" he asked.

A couple of hours had passed since their getaway from the *bandido* hideout. They had ridden hard since then, pushing their mounts for all they were worth. Their route had taken them east, the way Daniels had told Angelina to go when he headed back to help Buffalo.

There had been no sign of pursuit so far, and tracking anyone through these rugged, rocky mountains would be very difficult. They had put enough distance between themselves and the stronghold to be able to breathe a little easier now.

Buffalo leaned forward, easing himself in the saddle as he answered Daniels's question. "I figgered if Rafael saw me leavin', he'd try to stop me. So I set up a dis-traction ahead o' time. When I was in that hut where they had their powder and cartridges stored, I left a long fuse burnin'. Figgered if nobody stopped me, I could get on my mule, stop by there on my way out of the place, and snuff it out. If I didn't get back in time, though, it would likely be 'cause I was havin' trouble." He shrugged his massive shoulders. "You seen how it worked out."

"You knew Rafael would try to stop you because of the gold," Daniels said flatly. "What gold, dammit?"

"The gold that Guerrero stole from me back at Angelina's daddy's cantina," Buffalo snapped. "He'd already spent damn near half of it, but I wasn't goin' to let that other half get away. The same night Rafael killed Guerrero, I went lookin' and found what was left of the gold. I moved it from where Guerrero had it hid and stashed it in a hidey-hole of my own. Rafael must've heard about it from some of Guerrero's men, and when he saw me headin' out with those heavy saddlebags, he figgered out I had what was left."

Daniels shook his head. "But where did it *come* from?"

Buffalo regarded him solemnly and said, "That's a mighty long story, and it ain't none o' your business, son. Let's just say it's mine and I ain't lettin' no *bandido* have it without a fight."

"A fight you got Angelina and me mixed up in," Daniels said angrily. Angelina reached out and put a hand on his arm, but he shook her off. "Blast it, what right did you have to do that?"

"Was you plannin' on stayin' there?" Buffalo asked in return.

"Well, no, but—"

"Then why don't you just figger I got you out a mite early and let it go at that?"

Angelina spoke up. "Please, Curtis. Señor Buffalo is right. We could not have stayed. We had already decided that. Now we can go back to San Cristóbal, just as we planned."

Daniels took a deep breath, realizing that she was making sense. After a moment, he shook his head and said quietly, "Not to San Cristóbal. Rafael is going to be looking for all three of us now. He'll figure that you and I were in on that business with the gold. He's liable to think that we might go to San Cristóbal, and he'll send men there. I don't want to bring any more trouble down on Father Vicente and his people."

"That's smart thinkin'," Buffalo said. He squinted into the north, then pointed in that direction. "You head that way, now, and you'll run into New Mexico Territory after a while. Lots of fine country there. Plenty of places where folks could make a fresh start."

Daniels peered toward the United States and grimaced, thinking about the charges hanging over his head. Angelina must have read his thoughts, because she touched his arm again and said softly, "From New Mexico we could go many places, Curtis. We could go far, far from Texas. But we could also find out about Callie."

Pain pulled at Daniels's chest. She was right. He had run away from the tragedy that had taken his wife and son from him. Even before the trouble with the law, he had deserted the only remaining member of his family, turning his back on Callie because of his own guilt and hurt, never even trying to help her. That was a pretty low-down thing to do, he thought.

And it was past time he tried to put it right.

He nodded. "All right," he said. "We'll go north. I'm not sure where we'll end up, but at least that's a start in the right direction."

Angelina smiled at him, and he put his hand over hers, squeezing for a moment. Then he turned to Buffalo and said, "What about you?"

The big man grinned. "Oh, I reckon me'n Stink'll mosey on down south a ways. I can dodge Rafael without much trouble. May not even bother to do that. If'n the boy wants to settle things with me, I ain't goin' to be too hard to find. Sorry, Angelina, but I may wind up havin' to kill him."

She reached out to him. "You are more precious to me than he ever could be, Señor Buffalo. Please . . . take care of yourself."

"Always do, señorita, always do." Buffalo sighed heavily, then opened one of the saddlebags. "Hell," he said as he reached inside, "folks just keep whittlin' down this here gold. You might as well take some of it, too.''

He brought out his hand and extended two dull yellow bars toward Daniels. The young Texan stared at them for a long moment. Finally, he was able to say, ''That's a lot of gold.''

''You're liable to need it. 'Sides, I got more. And a resourceful feller can always find a little money when he needs it. Now, here, take it.''

Daniels took the bars, frowning as he saw the letters *CSA* stamped into them. What the devil had Buffalo been doing in the middle of Mexico with a bag full of Confederate gold?

But as the big man lifted a hand in farewell and turned his mules to ride deeper into the mountains, Curtis Daniels reflected that maybe there were some questions you just shouldn't ask about the man called Buffalo Newcomb.

GREAT
STORIES
═ OF THE ═
AMERICAN
WEST II

Eighteen short stories from Western giants including:
Louis L'Amour●John Jakes●Evan Hunter
●Jack London● Erle Stanley Gardner
●Loren D. Estleman●Chad Oliver
and eleven more!
Edited by Martin H. Greenberg
__0-425-15936-1/$6.99

─────────────────────────────────

Also available:
GREAT STORIES OF THE AMERICAN WEST
Edited by Martin H. Greenberg
__0-515-11840-0/$6.99

─────────────────────────────────

J.L. REASONER

__The Healer's Road   0-515-11762-5/$5.99

When his parents died because of a lack of proper medicine, Thomas Black vowed to become a doctor and better people's lives. Now, with the advent of war, he is challenged to provide better care than ever before–in a fraction of the time. During the savage conflict of the Civil War, Thomas Black, and his two children who follow in his footsteps, will embody the true nobility of the American spirit.

__Cossack Three Ponies   0-425-15666-4/$5.99

Sent to protect a delegation of Russian aristocrats on a goodwill mission, Viktor was thrilled to journey to the bold, open land of America. But when the arrogant nobles murdered an Indian for sport, Viktor knew that more blood would be shed.

Stranded in a foreign land and caught in a foreign war, with a mortal enemy at his side, Viktor set out to rescue a child from danger. To save his own life. And to become a Blackfoot legend...

__Under Outlaw Flags   0-425-16305-9/$5.99

Most folks thought the Wild West had faded into memory by 1917. But for the Tacker Gang, there was still plenty of opportunity to make a dishonest living in the wide-open spaces of a still-young country. Until the law caught up with them—and offered them a choice. Serve your country...or serve twenty years.

After a lawless life in the desert, the war in Europe was a whole new world. And it was wilder than anything they'd ever seen before...